YOU find the culprit!

103 Minute Mysteries challenge your powers to detect exactly where and how the criminal made his mistake.

Each mystery is short—about one minute's reading time. If you think you know the solution turn to the next page. There you will find the clue that Professor Fordney found.

Who is Professor Fordney?

A master detective—the expert the police call for their most puzzling cases.

You will find that Minute Mysteries are crossword puzzles in crime.

Test your ability to think!

Minute Mysteries

Austin Ripley

PERENNIAL LIBRARY

Harper & Row, Publishers

New York, Hagerstown,

San Francisco, London

This book was originally published in 1949 by Pocket Books, Inc. It is here reprinted by arrangement with Opera Mundi, Inc.

First PERENNIAL LIBRARY edition published 1976.

LIBRARY OF CONGRESS CATALOG CARD NUMBER: 76—10095

STANDARD BOOK NUMBER: 06—080387—8

77-03

Minute Mysteries

The squad car rocketed through the Chicago night. "You're too late," said the calm young man in room 409. Fordney gestured. Everett Moore, assistant treasurer of the Imperial Ice Cream Company, continued: "We had an unusually large collection tonight. At 1:30 I heard someone coming up the steps. Believing I was alone in the building, I hurriedly switched off the lights and tiptoed to the inner office. It was pitch dark there too. Someone entered with a flashlight. A streetcar was approaching and I waited until its noise covered the sound, then hastily dialed headquarters, whispered, 'Help. Room 409, 18 South Birch,' and left the receiver off. I went back to the connecting door—I'd left it open a crack. The flashlight was on the table and as the figure bent over it, I could see it was a masked man. Holding a gun in his hand he scraped the money from the table into a bag. A little runt he was, but I was unarmed. He beat it. I waited a couple of minutes, then turned on the lights."

"What number did you dial?" Fordney asked.

"Why, police headquarters—Police 1313."

The Professor observed a paper bag in the wastebasket. "Been out at all tonight?"

"Yes, for a sandwich and coffee at 11:15."

"Why didn't you eat in the restaurant?"

"I always bring my lunch back. Don't like to be gone too long."

"Get your hat," the Professor ordered. "We'll find out who your accomplice is at headquarters."

What single clue told Fordney that Moore was lying; that it was an inside job? Turn page for solution.

"The murderer climbed up to Lord Melford's opened bedroom window all right," insisted Detective Sergeant Boland, addressing Professor Fordney. "We discovered, you know, that all the entrance doors were locked on the inside and all the windows but the one in question were fastened. See those footprints in the flower bed?"

The two men were standing directly below his lordship's window when the Scotland Yard man grasped Fordney's arm in excitement and pointed to the ivy-covered wall of the old mansion. Ten feet from the ground, and leading to Melford's window on the third floor, the leaves were stripped and broken. "See, Professor, I was right! That's how the murderer did get in. Let's have another look inside."

Lord Melford lay on his bed, his throat cut, the pillow and spread covered with blood. One arm dangled over the edge. The night lamp was still burning. Walking to the open window, Boland discovered fresh scratches on the outside sill.

"That clinches it, Professor. Gosh I'd like to find you wrong just once! Your theory that it's an inside job and that the murderer did not make his entrance by the window is all shot now. The only one to gain by Melford's death is his nephew and—I don't believe he'd have the courage for a job like this."

Solution — Incident of the Calm Young Man

Fordney knew Moore was lying when he said he hastily dialed Police 1313 in the dark. Try dialing hastily in the dark. None but the blind, and those similarly trained, can dial successfully an unfamiliar number without seeing the dial.

THERE IS NO DARKNESS BUT IGNORANCE — Shakespeare

"Appearances are deceiving, old fellow—you've learned that. I'm really surprised that you've overlooked such a significant fact." Fordney carefully examined the window sill. "Do you see what I mean?"

What was the significant fact that Boland overlooked? Turn page for solution.

• • THE MYSTIC SOLVES HIS MURDER • •

The room was a shambles. A bullet wound in his head, famed Indian mystic, Haroun Bey, lay sprawled on the floor. Nearby was a nondescript brown single-breasted sports coat. In the dead man's hand was a button which Bey had torn from the garment while, thought Fordney, he and his assailant struggled for possession of the weapon. In tearing off the button a hole had been made in the coat's left side. After killing the seer his murderer had started to search the seance room but had been interrupted, perhaps surprised, and had hastily left. Such at least were the Professor's deductions.

Had the killer found what he was looking for? If so, what was it?

Three people were known to have visited Bey that evening.

At 7:30 socially-prominent Ida Pettinelli had called. Fordney learned she had a score to settle with the seer because he had revealed to her husband (for a substantial sum) a jealously guarded secret.

At 8:45 Attorney James Ross, whose name had been mentioned as the next governor, visited Bey. A few days before, the Indian had threatened to make public (unless paid for silence) an incident which would ruin his career.

At 9:10 Ira Hogan was admitted. Upon Bey's advice

he had invested heavily in a crooked scheme which back-fired and had lost everything. A pauper, health gone, spirit broken, Hogan had sworn vengeance.

Professor Fordney established definitely that Bey was alive at 7:30, the hour of his first evening appointment. All three suspects refused to talk; each disclaimed any knowledge of the murder. An incriminating paper concerning Ross was missing from Bey's room.

Reviewing the evidence, Fordney detained one of the three for further investigation.

Whom did Fordney suspect? Why? Turn page for solution.

• • • AN INTERRUPTED WEEKEND • • •

Professor Fordney, driving along a busy thoroughfare, suddenly slammed on the brakes and brought his car to a stop. He had just passed a huddled form lying in the street. Running back to the spot, he bent over a woman

---

Solution — A Significant Fact

As the ivy was broken only to within ten feet from the ground it was obvious that the murderer had made his exit, and not entrance, by way of the wall. Had he climbed up to the window the ivy would have been broken close to the ground. He could not possibly have gotten a foothold otherwise.

O. CREDULITY — Mason

---

about 50 years of age, clad in house dress and sweater, an ugly bruise on her forehead. That she was beyond help was quickly apparent to him; the body was cold, death having undoubtedly been caused by a car which left the marks of two tires across her chest.

Fordney instructed one of the officers, keeping the hastily drawn crowd back, to phone headquarters. An hour later the Professor was still trying to locate someone who might throw light on the tragedy.

After tedious and patient inquiry he learned the woman was a Mrs. Belamy, who lived on the outskirts of the town. The police finally located Nick Chester, a boarder of the dead woman's, who readily admitted having driven her downtown in his car. He said she'd got out two blocks from where Fordney had discovered her. On learning Mrs. Belamy had not been wearing glasses when found, Chester suggested she must have stepped in front of a car and the driver sped on.

The Professor sighed. He was not to find relief from the city heat this weekend! Well, his work came first.

"Now why was Mrs. Belamy wearing a man's sweater? And why has her body been thrown out at this particular spot? She certainly wasn't run over or killed there!" he muttered to himself disconsolately.

How did the Professor know? Turn page for solution.

• • • • • • **BEBE'S BAUBLES** • • • • • •

"Oh! Who . . . what are you . . ."

"Give me the key to your jewel case and keep moving —towards the bathroom," ordered the grim-faced young man who had silently entered the hotel suite of movie starlet Bebe Bedeaux.

"But . . . but . . ." spluttered the terrified Bebe.

"I wouldn't like to smash your pretty nose with this rod," said the gunman, "but unless you hand me that key I'll ruin your future before it starts! Thanks—now into the bathroom!"

* * *

"So, of course I went in," Bebe told Professor Fordney. "Just before I did so another man entered the suite. He wore a hat, and a handkerchief over his face. I was locked in the bathroom. When the maid let me out an hour later, my jewels were gone. Please, please get them back for me."

Studying the hotel registrations and questioning employees, the criminologist narrowed down the suspects to Burton Chance, Dick Lyon and Peter Drake. Further in-

---

Solution — The Mystic Solves His Murder

The Professor detained Ida Pettinelli. The button torn from the coat found on the floor, and clasped in the mystic's hand, left a hole on the left side of the coat. Only women's coats have buttons on the left side.

THE WAY OF THE WORLD IS TO MAKE LAWS, BUT FOLLOW CUSTOMS — Montaigne

---

Solution — An Interrupted Weekend

The weather was hot, yet Fordney found the woman's body cold. As she lay on a busy street and a body does not cool for at least several hours after death, he knew she had been killed elsewhere.

SCIENCE WHEN WELL DIGESTED IS NOTHING BUT GOOD SENSE AND REASON — Stanislaus

vestigation revealed that one of the three was the gunman who herded Bebe into the bathroom; one had been this man's partner in crime for many years; the third was a hotel employee. By chance Fordney discovered that it was the hotel employee who suggested the theft to the two crooks though he did not know they were professional jewel thieves. The only other information Fordney could immediately secure was the following:

1. Burton Chance had registered from Lima, Peru.
2. Dick Lyon and the gunman, both of whom were blond, had served time in London for jewel thievery and blackmail.
3. This was the hotel employee's first criminal venture.

Who was the gunman? Turn page for solution.

• • • • **DEATH BEATS THE BAND** • • • •

Removing the tottering razor from the edge of the wash basin, the Professor unsheathed its straight blade and observed its two nicks.

He stooped to the naked body of Paul Loken on the bathroom floor and carefully re-examined the ghastly slash in his throat which extended almost from ear to ear. The marks of one nick showed clearly.

The corpse wore only a single sock. The left hand clutched a scrap of sheet music. Doctor Graham sniffed a cigarette stub near the body. "Marijuana," he said. The two went to the living room.

"After the show, Nan, here—our singer—she has an

7

apartment two floors above—stopped by with Paul and me for a night cap," explained bandleader Cedric Kendrick. "Paul's our trumpet player—we share this apartment. Paul finished his drink and went to his room. About fifteen minutes later we heard a thud in the bathroom. We opened the door and . . . God! . . . what a ghastly sight! We didn't—we couldn't go in! I closed the door and phoned Doctor Graham and the police."

"Did you observe smoke in the bathroom?"

"Yes, a haze of reefer smoke. Paul was a marijuana addict."

"Did he suffer much?" asked Nan.

"Hardly at all," replied Doctor Graham, recalling the deep gash from left to right. "In some instances the victim lives long enough to do incredible things"—he glanced at Fordney—"but Loken died before he hit the floor—instantly."

"Which—among other things," added the Professor, "makes it murder! You both are under arrest."

What clue proved one of them (Kendrick) had murdered Loken? Turn page for solution.

Solution — Bebe's Baubles

1. As the hotel employee is not Burton Chance, he is either Lyon or Drake.
2. Tells us that Dick Lyon is not the gunman. Therefore, as we see in
3. That the hotel employee had no criminal record (and that he is not Lyon), the hotel employee was Peter Drake. Hence, as Drake had no criminal record and the gunman had, the gunman is Burton Chance.

Professor Fordney completed his examination of the room. Finding everything as it should be except for the body, and blood on the floor and window sill, he turned to the man sitting dumbly in the chair.

When questioned, the man recounted the tragedy.

"Several times tonight my wife was alarmed by noises outside the house and asked me to investigate. I did, but finding nothing wrong, I put it down to some jokester trying to frighten us.

"We went to bed at 1 o'clock and some time later I was awakened by a scraping noise and a low voice. In a few seconds my eyes became accustomed to the darkness and I made out a figure standing at the window. Reaching for my gun which was under the pillow, I fired twice, jumped up, turned on the light, and was horrified to see my wife lying there—dead. I phoned Dr. Willard and then . . ."

"Just a moment," broke in Fordney. "What did your examination show, doctor?"

"One bullet passed through the shoulder, the other entered the back, passed through the heart and emerged from the left breast. Death was practically instantaneous," the physician replied.

"Touch anything but the body, doctor?"

"Nothing."

"And you, Danlley?"

"Why . . . only the telephone. Then it was so cold . . . I . . . I . . . went to the cellar and built up the fire in the furnace."

"And a hot one you made, indeed," interrupted the Professor, raising the room's single window to let in some air. "A very stupidly planned crime, Danlley. Arrest him, Sergeant!"

Why? Turn page for solution.

• • • • • AT THE CROSS ROAD • • • • •

Brown, the taxi driver, pointed to the body of a dead man sitting upright in the center of the back seat. "This stiff was talkin' to a dame in front of the Hotel Burch when I pulled up there and delivered a passenger.

"He hailed me as I was about to shove off, and tole me to drive him to the Burlington cross road. I knew the shortest way, but the skirt tells me to take a longer route over the old bumpy road and when he says O. K., I did it. That's why it took me so long to get there."

"Go on," said Professor Fordney.

"Honest to God, mister, I don't know how he got that knife in his heart. I didn't stop once—beat every light in the city and when I drew up at the cross road and he made no move to get out, I turned around and saw that knife stickin' in him! There was a pole-light right there so I could see plainly.

"I just felt his pulse, then I beat it for headquarters—

Solution — Death Beats the Band

Loken died instantly. Had he cut his own throat, therefore, the open razor would have fallen to the floor, but Fordney found it lying on the edge of the wash basin closed!

GUILTINESS WILL SPEAK THOUGH TONGUES WERE OUT OF USE — *Shakespeare*

---

fast. I knew he was dead. I've seen plenty of stiffs in my time. But how that knife got in his heart, unless he stabbed himself, I don't know."

"Was the lady tall or short?"

"Short and thin . . . but a nice lookin' bit . . ."

"Was the passenger you delivered to the hotel a woman?"

"Yeah . . . an old dame . . ."

"You're lying, Brown, so I'm going to hold you," interrupted the Professor.

How did Fordney know Brown was lying? Turn page for solution.

• • • • • • **CLASS DAY** • • • • • •

"Some of you seniors will remember Ed Krause who graduated a couple of years ago," Fordney said to his class. "Well, I met Ed last night—he's an FBI Special Agent—and he had an experience recently that I'm sure will interest you fellows.

"Krause and his colleague, George Hoffman, worked as farm hands on the farm of Otto Shendrik and Honus Wenger, both suspected of subversive activities. One day Shendrik's actions made it imperative that Ed contact Hoffman at a previously arranged rendezvous. So that evening at sunset he was stricken with a terrific toothache and asked Shendrik if he could drive his car to the general store for medication.

"The suspicious and penurious farmer agreed—if Ed paid for the gas. The general store was exactly 6½ lonely miles due north of the farm and Shendrik said he got exactly 13 miles to the gallon of gas. Well, after Shendrik noted the mileage on the speedometer, Krause paid him for a gallon. Shendrik warned him not to go a foot beyond the store! He wasn't a goin' to have his tires worn out traipsin' about!

"What a dilemma for Ed! He had to show up at the store—Shendrik might check—but his meeting place was 2 miles east on a road 1 mile south of the store. And he didn't know how to disconnect or alter the speedometer. If it showed over 13 miles of travel Ed knew he would be dismissed. Yet he had to contact Hoffman!

"Ed's smart," concluded the Professor, "and was equal to the occasion. He drove to the store, to his rendezvous with Hoffman and back to the farm. He didn't touch the speedometer (nor did anyone else), yet when Shendrik checked it registered exactly 13 additional miles. How did Krause manage it?"

How did he? Turn page for solution.

Solution — A Horrible Mistake

Had the tragedy occurred as related by Danlley, at least one of the bullets, which passed through the body, would have broken the window which Fordney found closed.

NO WICKEDNESS HAS ANY GROUND OF REASON — Livy

Solution — At the Cross Road

It would have been physically impossible for the body of a dead man to have been sitting upright in the center of the seat especially when the taxi drove over an old bumpy road.

THERE ARE COUNTLESS ROADS ON ALL SIDES TO THE GRAVE — Cicero

The alarm went out. The widespread net soon brought up some choice underworld fish. Professor Fordney left his laboratory at midnight and went to headquarters to assist homicide chief, Inspector James A. Kelley. A notorious gangland big-shot had been cut to ribbons and his body dumped on his doorstep in a bold challenge to the police.

Those questioned were grim and silent. Both Kelley and Fordney refused information to the press other than the following:

Being held are seven criminals, among them the leader and the actual killer. They are Eli Rickel, gambler; Sylvester Zych, ward politician; Rudolph Vock, ex-convict; Ned Baskin, bodyguard; Monte Montalto, the slot-machine king; Eddie Croft, labor racketeer; and Joe Gorski, wrestler.

1. Eli Rickel, Monte Montalto, and the killer are the most ruthless of the seven. Fordney believes them responsible for at least four unsolved murders in the past seven months.

2. Rudolph Vock, and the leader, and Joe Gorski were tried for the San Francisco murder of Big Jake Kilroy and acquitted.

3. Sylvester Zych and the killer were such close friends that they recently aroused the suspicions of Vock and Gorski who reported them to the leader.

4. The killer and Ned Baskin were partners in a numbers racket. Baskin has a glass eye. The killer is believed to have a fortune in Brazilian banks.

5. The leader and Montalto each has a moll in the chorus of a hit musical.

6. The leader and Eddie Croft recently made an "observational" trip to Mexico City.

7. Eli Rickel and the leader did a stretch together at Waupun State Prison.

Who is the gang leader? Turn page for solution.

• • • • • • **POOR DISGUISE** • • • • • •

"Anne . . . Oh . . . Oh . . . Anne!" shrieked Rudolph Shepard, staring at his wife. "She's killed herself!" Hearing his cries, Christopher Newcome, his employer, rushed to the servants' quarters. The pillow on which Anne's head rested was covered with blood that streamed from a bullet hole in her temple.

"Leave the gun where it is . . . don't touch anything," commanded Newcome. "I'll phone the police."

"Get a doctor, sir," pleaded the servant.

"No use . . . she is dead."

When Inspector Kelley and the Professor arrived they found Rudolph kneeling beside his wife's bed, weeping.

"Who discovered her?" demanded Kelley.

"I did, sir," he sobbed.

Solution — Class Day

Krause drove the distance from the main road to his meeting place and back to the main road backwards! Speedometers do not register backward mileage.

THE MARCH OF INTELLECT WHICH LICKS THE WHOLE WORLD INTO SHAPE — Goethe

---

"Can't understand how she got my gun!" exclaimed Newcome as Kelley picked it up from the bed.

"You remember, sir, you said it wasn't working properly? I brought it up to my room to fix it. I removed a piece of grit beneath the ejector and forgot to put it back in your room."

Fordney observed a maid's uniform and a nightgown on a chair beside the bed. Pulling back the covers his attention was drawn to a long, recently-made scratch running diagonally across the woman's chest. She had removed only her shoes and uniform. On the back of both hands, clenched to her sides, were small dark bruises.

While Rudolph was explaining the presence of the gun Fordney saw that Kelley realized it was murder and not suicide.

When did he? Turn page for solution.

. . . . . **A RECENT STICK-UP** . . . . .

After an epicurean dinner, Professor Fordney and several of his cronies were seated in the lounge of the club.

"Now then," said the criminologist, "if you crime fans insist on having me give you a criminal case in which there is only one error, here you are." He handed the following newspaper clipping to Charles Winters, a well-known business man of Danbury.

PARKED DRIVER SLAIN AT SIDE OF WOMAN FRIEND

Opens Sedan Window to Gunman's Tap, Is Shot Before Getting Hands Up

A man tapped on the closed window of a car in which

Joseph Candora, a highway contractor's helper, from Bridgeport, Conn., and Mrs. Rose Worth, a telephone operator, of 62 East 127th Street, were sitting early yesterday morning at 187th Street and Riverside Drive. Candora raised the window and the man, a stranger to Mrs. Worth, thrust a pistol through the aperture and announced it was a stick-up.

Candora, Mrs. Worth said later, made no move to resist the gunman, but the intruder, almost as he made his an-

---

Solution — The Unholy Seven

Eli Rickel is neither the killer (1) nor the leader (7). Rudolph Vock is neither leader (2) nor killer (3). Sylvester Zych is neither leader nor killer (3). Monte Montalto is neither the killer (1) nor the leader (5). Joe Gorski is neither the leader (2) nor the killer (3). Ned Baskin is eliminated only as the killer (4). Eddie Croft is eliminated only as the leader (6). Therefore Ned Baskin is the leader and Eddie Croft the killer.

I AM A FOOL, I KNOW IT! — Congreve

Solution — Poor Disguise

Fordney knew it was murder the moment he entered the room. The girl's hands were clenched close to her sides under the covers. If she had shot herself, at least one hand would have been outside. Also the long scratch across her chest and the bruises on her hands indicated a struggle before she was killed.

EVEN THE FOOL IS WISE AFTER THE EVENT — Homer

nouncement, pressed the trigger of his weapon. The bullet struck Candora in the throat and he fell forward, fatally wounded. Detectives of the Wadsworth Avenue police station believe it was a deliberate murder. The killer got into another automobile, in which two men awaited him, and was driven away. Mrs. Worth raced down the drive, screaming.

Winters read intently after which he snorted, "That's easy, Professor."

What is factually wrong with the newspaper account? Turn page for solution.

Turn page for solution.

• • AFFAIR OF THE QUICK DEDUCTION • •

Detective-Sergeant Tom Conroy's cherubic expression of satisfaction leaped to one of blazing wrath—and humiliation—as he listened in his hotel room to the dictagraph he had planted in the adjoining suite. Notorious but never-convicted jewel thief Derek Jason was talking to his brilliant wife, Lily Lomez.

"And so, my sweet, as the gendarmes are showing faint traces of intelligence we must separate—temporarily."

"But what," asked Lily, "about the Brandon job?"

"It will go through as planned. I won't decide for several days where and when, but I'll let you know in time to arrange our getaway."

Lily's voice was puzzled. "But how shall I know, when you say we mustn't meet, wire, telephone or telegraph each other?"

"That," laughed Derek, "is what our detective friend in the next room would give his bow-legged mother-in-law away to know! Here—read this, then I'll burn it."

* * *

"We've tailed them every minute, Professor," Sergeant Conroy continued. "We've got a tap on both their phones, and mail and wires of each are covered. They have not seen each other but I'm positive Jason's going to pull the Brandon job and Lily arrange the getaway. How are we going to head them off?"

Fordney was silent for several minutes. Finally, "Do they both bank at the same place?"

"Yes. First National. Funny thing too. Jason makes a deposit every morning, and in the afternoon Lily makes a withdrawal."

The criminologist bustled out of his chair. "Come along, Sergeant! Perhaps we'll not be too late to forestall the clever Jason!"

Can you deduce Jason's and Lily's means of daily communication? Turn page for solution.

Turn page for solution.

Solution — A Recent Stick-up

A man tapped on the closed window of a car, yet the victim raised the window and the gunman thrust a pistol through the aperture and announced it was a stick-up!

Had the window been closed Candora could not have raised it. Had it been moved at all it would have been lowered.

ANY MAN MAY COMMIT A MISTAKE — Cicero

It was a bizarre sight. Tiny, exotically beautiful Mado Gougin hung from an arm of the heavy chandelier, her legs dangling through an opening in the dining room table. She was dressed for the street in dainty high-heeled slippers, short skirt and green silk blouse.

The three leaves that had been removed from the center of the highly polished table stood against a wall. The inexpert knot barely held. The rope was slight and had stretched considerably; Mado's feet were but an inch from the floor.

The wealthy Mado, a child musical prodigy who had never quite fulfilled the promise of youth, had been an extreme exhibitionist.

Why she had married stodgy Herbert Ashley was a mystery to her friends.

The mild-mannered Ashley was talking:

"I'm afraid that young Major Redfield's death caused this. He was killed in the Pacific recently. Yes, I know Mado was in love with him, but"—he shrugged deprecatingly—"genius has license denied us lesser humans. I returned from hunting an hour ago and found her as she is. She was alone—she dismissed all the servants last week—considered it patriotic. . . ."

"The only marks on the table, Professor, are the woman's fingerprints and a single drop of wax, but there is face powder and a rouge streak as well as her prints on the leaves." Sergeant Bell looked curiously at Ashley and continued: "We found a scale in the kitchen. She weighs exactly 101 pounds. Shall I book Ashley for murder, sir?"

Fordney nodded.

Why did Fordney believe Ashley had murdered his wife? Turn page for solution.

When private detectives Buck Merrick and Sid Damon attempted to push their way into apartment 302 of the Rensonia, they were met with a hail of bullets by the four men who dashed from the apartment. Merrick dropped with four slugs in his body and died shortly afterwards without identifying his slayer.

Damon told Professor Fordney that he and Merrick, working for wealthy oil man John Wright, finally located

---

Solution — Affair of the Quick Deduction

Derek and Lily had a joint safe deposit box. Each morning Derek would leave a note in it advising Lily of his progress; each afternoon she would read it, and leave her own concerning plans for the getaway. Fordney secured the necessary authorization to open the box so he knew Jason's and Lily's plans well in advance. Simple, what?

FOR HER OWN BREAKFAST SHE'LL PROJECT A SCHEME NOR TAKE HER TEA WITHOUT A STRATAGEM — Young

---

Solution — Incident of the Exhibitionistic Corpse

Had Mado stood on the table (straddling the opening made by the missing leaves as she would have had to do, had she hanged herself, the table would have been scratched by her high heels. The only marks on it, however, were her fingerprints and the wax, proving the table had been placed in position after she had been hanged.

MEN ARE OF NECESSITY SO MAD, THAT NOT TO BE MAD, WERE MADNESS IN ANOTHER FORM — Pascal

the hideout of the con gang who had fleeced their client of $35,000, and attempted to bring them in. While he was new on the case, Merrick had told him the mob comprised Oswald Munson, Dan Carmody, Rick Somer and Handsome Harry Keeler.

His wound dressed, Damon and the Professor went deep into the underworld to secure the following additional information:

1. One of the four, a former professor of Romance languages, was the mob's front.
2. Somer had been trying to gain the confidence of the former professor (for some secret reason of his own) but the front did not trust him.
3. The molls of Carmody and the front were Handsome Harry Keeler's beautiful sisters.
4. The front and the man who killed Merrick were close pals, and both have records in Australia.
5. After the mob's last successful job, Keeler and Merrick's slayer split $2000 more than the other two members because of expenses they had incurred.

Sifting their information, Damon and Fordney quickly identified the killer and broadcast an alarm. He was picked up three days later boarding a plane.

Who killed Buck Merrick? Turn page for solution.

With a heroic heave Sergeant Cargo forced Andrew Morse's library door. The aged philanthropist sat at his desk—dead. On a small table stood a whisky decanter (stopper freshly nicked), tall glass almost empty, bowl of ice cubes, bottle of spring water (no cap), stoppered with a tiny cork, and a small empty vial. On a desk was a small card bearing the typewritten words, DROWNED IN THE SEA OF FUTILITY.

The Professor toyed with his ear, then walked across to the open French doors leading to a terrace. An outside thermometer read 20 degrees above.

In the kitchen Anna, Morse's old housekeeper, told her brief story.

"I took the master whisky at 9:30—the usual hour—but he seemed nervous and unwell, so 20 minutes ago I rapped to see if he were all right. When he didn't answer I telephoned you, Professor."

As Fordney descended the front steps Morse's nephew, Ted Terry, stepped from a taxi. The time was 11:14.

"I've bad news for you, son. We found your uncle dead in the library—poisoned."

Solution — Con Gang Killer

First, let's discover the front. He is not Somer (2) or Keeler or Carmody (3), hence the front is Oswald Munson. The front (Munson) is not the killer (4). The killer is not Somer (2 & 4) and we see in (5) that Keeler is not the murderer. Therefore, Dan Carmody is the man who killed Merrick.

GO BACK; THE VIRTUE OF YOUR NAME IS NOT HERE PASSABLE — Shakespeare

"Poisoned? Poisoned? How ghastly! But why was the library door locked? Was Uncle afraid of someone?"

"No, I think not—the French doors were open. Been to the fights?"

"No. I've been working all evening in the office."

"Couldn't you get a seat?"

"Oh, yes. I had a ringside one." Terry held out a ticket. "Up to the last minute I thought perhaps I'd make it, but . . ."

Fordney shivered, re-entered the house. An unpleasant task was ahead of him.

Whom did Fordney suspect? Why? Turn page for solution.

• • • • • • **AMBUSHED** • • • • • •

"We'd better walk here on the side, John," Fordney said as they started along the only path to the woods.

Trudging along, John said, "As I told you, Professor, Crane left the lodge to go hunting. About ten minutes later, I heard a shot and a scream. I ran down the path and found him about five hundred yards from the house, bleeding terribly from a wound in the head. I dashed back for the first-aid kit and bandaged him as best I could, but he died before I finished. Then I went back to the lodge and phoned you."

Reaching the spot where Crane lay, he explained, "I turned him over so that I could dress his head."

"He must have been shot from ambush, as there are no other footprints about but those in the path, three sets of which are yours, the other Crane's," the Professor said after a careful examination.

Walking into the underbrush, he exclaimed, "The murderer must have stood near here. See those powder marks on the leaves of this branch?"

While cutting off the branch Fordney gashed his hand. "Better sterilize that," John suggested.

Back at the lodge, Fordney was about to pick up a bottle of Zonite from the kit John had used when he observed a dark brown spot on the label. Walking to the basin, he looked in the mirror above it, and saw John furtively slip a pair of scissors into the kit.

Turning around slowly, he said, "I'm going to hold you on suspicion of murder!"

Why? Turn page for solution.

• • • • • •　　CASE 463　　• • • • • •

At 8:10 P.M., July 4, 1945, Miss Ruby Marshall left her apartment on the fifth floor of the Hotel Oakwood. As she walked toward the elevator she passed Jane McGuire. The fourteen-year-old child had her Scottish terrier on a long leash and as they came opposite each other the dog growled and leaped at Miss Marshall. The woman screamed and ran back to her apartment.

Thirty minutes later Mrs. McGuire had a call from police headquarters informing her that Miss Marshall had received first aid at Mercy Hospital for a wound on the

---

Solution — Fate and Futility

Terry said he had been at the office all evening, yet he knew that the library door was locked; a fact he could not possibly have known without guilty knowledge.

BE SURE YOUR SIN WILL FIND YOU OUT — Holy Bible

knee where the McGuire dog had bitten her. Invalided for the past two years, Mrs. McGuire was unable to look into the situation herself. She immediately called her friend, Professor Fordney, informing him of the above and asking him to look into the matter.

He found Miss Marshall sitting on a chair in the emergency ward, about to leave the hospital. Receiving permission to examine the wound from the doctor who had just taken care of her, Fordney raised Miss Marshall's immaculate evening dress, noticed her hose were rolled below her knees, removed the bandage and found cauterized marks on the right knee cap. Turning to the physician he inquired, "Are you sure those are teeth marks?"

"Why . . . they look like it to me!"

Lowering the woman's dress, the Professor told her, "You certainly didn't show much intelligence in trying to frame this charge against Mrs. McGuire, toward whom you hold a personal grudge. Her dog did not bite you!"

How did he know? Turn page for solution.

• • • • • •   CLASS DAY   • • • • • •

"I had hoped," Fordney said to his class some years ago, "to have the great physicist, Professor Albert Einstein, who first promulgated the theory of relativity in 1905, here to talk to you chaps today. Unfortunately he cannot be present, so I shall tell you of an exploit of another famed scientist, Sir Joshua Beckwith, Professor of Hierology in London.

"He had uncovered an ancient tomb in Egypt and, through his undisputed knowledge and ability to read hieroglyphics, had definitely established the date of the birth and the reign of a great Pharaoh whose mummy he had discovered. A man of volatile temper, and emphatic scientific views which he did not hesitate to express in exposing charlatanism, he had many enemies.

"The British Museum soon received a message, signed by Sir Joshua, which in part read as follows: 'Have discovered the tomb of an important Pharaoh who reigned from 1410 to 1428 B.C. and who died at the age of 42 years, leaving two sons and two daughters. Great wealth found in sarcophagus. One of his sons died shortly after his reign began, etc. . . .!'

"The Museum officials at first were astonished," continued Fordney, "but examination of the communication quickly told them it was either a very stupid fake or an attempt at a 'practical joke'!

"They were right in their belief that the message did not come from Sir Joshua Beckwith. He did make a most

---

Solution — Ambushed

There were three sets of John's footprints on the path. Had he been at the lodge when his friend was shot, and made two trips to the body and back, there would have been four sets. He later confessed he was in the woods and killed Crane as he passed. In his excitement and anxiety to shield himself he overlooked the importance of the missing set of footprints.

THAT IS TO BE WISE TO SEE THAT WHICH LIES BEFORE YOUR FEET — Terence

---

Solution — Case 463

Fordney knew the dog had not bitten Miss Marshall because he found no teeth marks in the dress. She later confessed to inflicting the wound herself with a fork in the hope of collecting damages from Mrs. McGuire.

---

important discovery—but how did the Museum authorities know the communication was not authentic?"

How did they know? Turn page for solution.

• • • • • • **THE BREAK** • • • • • • •

Four tough prisoners in the county jail tore plumbing from the wall, beat two guards with iron pipes, brutally killing one, and escaped through a hole in the wall, after arming themselves with guns and ammunition. They were Dan Morgan, Sam Chapin, Louis Segal and Anton Kroll, all being held for armed robbery.

A posse was quickly organized and the gang surrounded in a small valley fifteen miles from the jail. Two of the mob were wounded and all captured, but not before one of the gang killed State Trooper Don Burton with a bullet through his head.

Professor Fordney interrogated the sullen four separately but each refused any information concerning himself or the others. From outside sources, however, the criminologist learned the following facts.

1. An erstwhile dancer, one of the four, acted as a front for the gang. He spoke several languages fluently.
2. For some time the ugly Segal and the handsome front had been suspicious of each other.
3. A week before their arrest, Sam Chapin and the front won $4,000 each in a crap game at Anton Kroll's lake cabin. Kroll does not gamble.
4. The front and the prisoner who killed Trooper Don Burton are good friends. They once ran a gambling house in Cuba.
5. Anton Kroll and the killer have been going with twin sisters who knew nothing of their criminal backgrounds.

Fordney sat in his study evaluating the above data. After a few moments he reached for the phone, called the prosecuting attorney and advised him to issue a murder warrant for . . .

Who killed Trooper Don Burton? Turn page for solution.

• • THE END OF A CRIMINAL CAREER • •

Fordney picked up the typewritten note which lay under Carr's head, slumped on the desk beside his typewriter. He read:

Field just called. He's coming to get me. I can't escape him. I'll be dead in five minutes. This will tell the police who did it. I hear him—he's coming in the door now. Th . . .

"Got him right through the heart," remarked the Professor, handing the note to Sergeant Reynolds.

"That's right," commented Reynolds. "He died instantly and didn't have time to finish the note. He was an unusual personality," the Sergeant continued. "What you'd call a pacifist among criminals. Never carried a gat and was proud of the fact that he'd never shed another's blood in

---

Solution — Class Day

The Museum authorities knew the communication was not an authentic one because of the manner of expressing the dates of the Pharaoh's reign. All B.C. dates, in the Christian calendar, are expressed in the reverse manner from A.D. dates, for obvious reasons. Thus, for example, Moses lived from 1571 to 1451 B.C. and Tutankhamen reigned from 1358 to 1350 B.C.

his long criminal career. I don't understand, though, why he just sat there and waited for death—even though he was paralyzed on the right side."

"Do you notice the odor in the room, Reynolds? Very fine perfume. It's faint but definite. Odd, isn't it?"

"I don't smell it. Guess my old beaker isn't as keen as yours."

"Odd—very odd," mused Fordney.

He noted the position of the body—facing the single door to the room. About ten feet in back of the dead man's chair was a single window, locked and heavily barred.

"My, that perfume's delightful," remarked the Professor, sniffing the air. "Well, another case of criminal stupidity, Sergeant," he added, feeling Carr's right arm. "I don't think Field did this job."

Reynolds looked puzzled.

Why didn't the Professor think so? Turn page for solution.

• • • •   **MILKMAN'S DISCOVERY**   • • • •

God! He hadn't meant to kill Anita! And if she hadn't insisted so on marriage, and threatened him . . . He raised the window quietly.

* * *

The Professor lifted his eyes from the twisted, broken, pajama-clad body lying a foot from the apartment building, looked quizically at milkman Horace Bone, who had discovered the tragedy at 5:30 that morning.

"From where did you phone the police?" he asked.

"From the janitor's apartment."

"Then you continued your milk deliveries throughout the building?"

"Yes. The janitor stayed by the body. Wasn't that all right?"

Fordney gazed up to the fourth floor balcony off of Anita Brownley's apartment, lowered his eyes to the third floor window of Cyril Morse's apartment, turned to the other man.

"Did you visit your fiancée last night?"

"No, no, I didn't," Morse replied.

"Yet you say you were home all evening. Isn't that a bit . . ."

"I didn't visit her, but Anita came down to my apartment for awhile. She left at 11 o'clock. No, I heard nothing during the night."

"Was the body disturbed in any way?" Fordney asked Bone.

"No, sir."

* * *

Solution — The Break

Before ascertaining the killer's identity we will find out who is the mob front.

The front is not Louis Segal (2). And he is not Anton Kroll or Sam Chapin (3), therefore the front is Dan Morgan. Dan Morgan (the front) is not the killer (4). The killer is not Louis Segal (2 and 4) and in (5) we learn Anton Kroll is not the murderer. Hence the man who killed Trooper Burton is Sam Chapin.

GO BACK; THE VIRTUE OF YOUR NAME IS NOT HERE PASSABLE — Shakespeare

Solution — The End of a Criminal Career

If Carr had been shot while writing the note he couldn't have removed it from the typewriter. His assassin wrote the note. In attempting to incriminate Field he made a fatal mistake.

EVERY FACT THAT IS LEARNING BECOMES A KEY TO OTHER FACTS — Yeomans

The Professor climbed through Anita's open window to the four-foot balcony off the two rear windows of her one-room apartment, scraped a fingernail along the low iron railing, looked up at the next balcony two floors above and murmured, "Quite."

He stepped back into the room. The word GOODBYE, cut from a magazine, was pasted on the dressing table mirror. He knew, of course, that Anita had not gone to her death from her apartment—and that spelled murder.

What clue told Fordney Anita had not jumped or fallen from her own apartment? Turn page for solution.

• • • • DEATH SET THE TABLE • • • •

The short-range charge had ripped away the right side of Norman Baker's face. On a kitchen table—standing two feet from the wall, lay the 12-gauge shotgun—its muzzle projecting over the table side—its stock weighted down by a sack of flour—that had ended Baker's life. Around the gun trigger was a thin cord, its end draped over the table's edge. Sidewise to the table stood a chair from which, apparently, Baker's body had fallen to the floor after the shotgun's discharge.

"I was coming up the path to the cottage when I heard the report," Sidney Taylor said. "When I got here Norm was lying as you see him. He must have tied the cord to the gun, then sat there and pulled the trigger."

"Any reason for suicide that you know of?"

"Well, he was quite despondent over the market."

The Professor's eyes traveled to the wall phone.

"I had it connected before we arrived," explained Taylor. "You see, this is my summer cottage. I've never hunted before but there's lots of game hereabouts, so when Norm continued to brood in the city, I suggested we come up here for awhile."

"Were you associated in business?"

"In a way. I backed his latest venture with $50,000."

The criminologist examined Taylor's gun. "Do any shooting today?"

"Yes,—a bit."

"Get any game?"

"No. I'm afraid I'm a very poor shot."

"But not," snapped Fordney, "poor enough to miss a human target at a foot or two—though you were badly rattled when you murdered your friend."

How did Fordney know Baker was not a suicide? Turn page for solution.

How did Fordney know Baker was not a suicide? Turn page for solution.

• • • • MURDER IN THE MIRROR • • • •

"I won't be a hypocrite and pretend a sorrow I do not feel," stated Mrs. Elsie Morley. "She tried her best to kill me."

Fordney picked up a sharp butcher knife near the body of Mrs. Morley's attractive daughter-in-law, Rachel, handed it to Sergeant Dodd. In silence he looked about

---

Solution — Milkman's Discovery

Anita's balcony off the two rear windows of her apartment was four feet wide. Hence had she jumped or fallen from there, her body could not have been one foot from the building. After killing the girl in his apartment (which obviously had no balcony) Morse dropped her from his window.

COMMON SENSE IS A RARE COMMODITY — Bovee

the cheerful kitchen. Three tins of cookies ready to be baked were on a table. On a counter was half-kneaded bread dough. He opened the oven door. The oven was warm and empty.

"Now, Mrs. Morley," he said gently.

"My son, Tommy, married Rachel six months ago. She was a coarse, common little thing. I did everything possible to put some decency and refinement into her, but"—she gestured wearily—"it was hopeless."

"I was trying to teach her to bake and upbraided her for her lack of interest when it happened. I glanced into the mirror over the sink and saw her pick up that knife and start toward me. 'I'll shut that nagging mouth of yours,' she shrieked. We struggled desperately for the knife. I finally got it away from her. She dashed toward me furiously and it caught her in the throat."

The Professsor looked into the sink mirror as Dodd entered and said:

"Both Mrs. Morley's and the girl's fingerprints are sharply outlined in the flour on the knife handle, but there's something else that . . ."

"Did you touch anything after you phoned the police?" Fordney asked.

"Only the stove."

Fordney sighed. "Why did you deliberately kill your daughter-in-law?"

What clue proved Mrs. Morley's story false? Turn page for solution.

In a clump of woods 100 yards off the isolated road Professor Fordney examined the dead bodies of two girls. Both, about twenty-seven years old, were well dressed and extremely attractive. Their clothes were torn and it was obvious there had been a terrific struggle. There was a single bullet in the brain of each girl, fired at very close range.

A mile distant, another girl of about the same age was found wandering in a dazed condition, suffering from shock and amnesia. Her hysterical speech had a British accent.

In a ditch on the road an abandoned car was found. From examination of the luggage Fordney knew it had been used by the three girls.

Diligent search of the girls' effects revealed only extremely meager information.

The girls were Louise Holden, Sandra Worth and Marie Rochelle. All were London school teachers and one of them, who apparently had spent two years in Calcutta, was

---

Solution — Death Set the Table

Baker could not possibly have discharged the gun by pulling the cord about the trigger. In its position it could have been discharged only by pushing the trigger. Taylor's inexperience with guns and feverish panic betrayed him.

FALSE AS A FOWLER'S ARTFUL SNARE — Smollett

Solution — Murder in the Mirror

Had Mrs. Morley and Rachel struggled for the knife, as the woman alleged, their fingerprints would have been blurred and smudged— not sharply outlined as they were.

STILL HARPING ON MY DAUGHTER — Shakespeare

proficient in Hindu dancing. They were in this country on a holiday, but evidently with a view to remaining if possible. The only other pertinent information secured from the girls' luggage and handbags was the following:

1. Sandra Worth and the Hindu dancer had agreed to remain in the States only if they secured a teaching assignment in the same school.

2. Louise Holden and the living girl suffering amnesia, had taught in London for five years, while the Hindu dancer had but recently completed her first year of teaching in England.

With the above information, Fordney quickly determined the identity of the living girl.

Who is she? Turn page for solution.

• • • • • **THE PEAL OF DOOM** • • • • •

"Here's to good old sappy Cecil!" laughed Inez Watson, raising her glass. "If he knew I was here he'd . . ."

The doorbell pealed.

"Just the delicatessen boy," Norton assured her.

The startled Norton opened the door to Cecil Watson who covered him. In Norton's living room Watson turned up the radio, pocketed his own gun, took Norton's from his desk and without a word crashed a bullet through Inez's heart.

Then he forced Norton to type and sign the following note:

Inez would not be unfaithful to Cecil, so I shot her. I am now going to kill myself. REX NORTON.

Ah! That was saving face!

A bullet nipped through Norton's brain. Watson was deadly calm—so he thought.

"On with the gloves," he muttered. "Raise the shade.

35

There. Turn down the radio. Now get Norton's prints on his own gun. That's it. Could use a drink, but . . . no . . . no mistakes now!"

Watson walked to the door, snapped off the lights and left.

* * *

Before the police entered the house, Watson explained to Fordney:

"I came here to kill them both. I knew Inez was here. I peeked under the window shade and to my amazement saw Norton shoot her, write something on the typewriter, then blast his brains out. I called headquarters and waited outside."

The Professor switched on the lights and for five minutes moved about the living room "getting the picture" in silence.

He handed Watson the note.

"Oh, my God!" cried Watson. "She wasn't unfaithful! Inez darling, I . . ."

"Take the murdering hypocrite along, Sergeant," barked Fordney.

What single clue inspired the Professor's order? Turn page for solution.

Solution — Who Am I?

Before identifying the living girl, let's first determine who the Hindu dancer is. In (1) we know she is not Sandra Worth and in (2) we see she is not Louise Holden—therefore the Hindu dancer-teacher is Marie Rochelle. Therefore, as Marie Rochelle is the dancer-teacher and Louise Holden and the living girl (2) had been teaching in England for five years, while Marie had taught only one year, neither Louise Holden nor Marie Rochelle is the living girl. Consequently the living girl suffering amnesia is Sandra Worth.

READ TO WEIGH AND CONSIDER — Bacon

Fordney faced the house as he stood at the outer edge of the wide flower bed. Along its edge were two ladder impressions. Between them and the house lay the twisted body of Henri Buton.

As the Professor raised his eyes to the window, he observed a woman in a green jacket furtively close a wall safe.

After inspecting the tall ladder that had been removed to some bushes, twenty feet distant, the criminologist entered the house, glanced into the living room and went to the roof.

"I was sketching up here"—white-sweatered artist Arvonne Buton indicated her easel—"while Henri—he is my uncle—and Alexis Randoff, my fiancé, pottered about painting the furniture, rearranging the flower boxes and building that bower over there."

Fordney examined the half-completed bower with interest as Arvonne continued:

"Henri called that he needed more nails and laths and started down the ladder. Suddenly he lost his balance, let out a terrible cry and . . . and . . . fell."

"If he hadn't broken his neck on that rock in the border he might not have been even seriously injured," Randoff added.

"How do you know his neck is broken?" the Professor asked.

"Why . . . I . . . could tell when I . . . I . . . tried to help him."

"Did you otherwise disturb the body?"

"No."

"Did you touch his body?"

"No . . . no . . . I couldn't," Arvonne sobbed.

37

"The ladder—why did you take that down?"

"I knocked it over in getting to Henri, so I just put it out of the way," Randoff explained.

The Professor observed a fresh scratch on Arvonne's face, said:

"Buton's death was no accident. You are both under arrest."

How did Fordney know Buton's death was not accidental? Turn page for solution.

• • • • • • CLASS DAY • • • • • •

"Well, boys," the Professor smiled genially, "how do you feel this morning after last night's banquet? I'm sure it was a real treat for you to hear those police chiefs." Fordney was talking to his class at the University.

"It's true that most of them were 'old-timers,' but in most cases, without the aid of science (which we know is a great help), Captain Gilbert was right. Intelligent and quick observation counts more in crime detection than anything else. I know I've often told you that," catching Bill in the act of nudging Jack, "and some of you have

---

Solution — The Peal of Doom

Watson only thought he was calm, normal. On leaving he switched off the living room lights, proving that Norton could not have done in the dark what Watson said he saw; also that even if Norton had, it would have been impossible for Watson to have witnessed his actions! Watson went to the chair.

CUNNING IS BUT THE LOW MIMIC OF REASON — Bolingbroke

---

profited, but others," looking Bill in the eye, "have discounted its significance! Today I'm going to give you a simple test in observation acumen.

"Most of you probably have a United States dollar bill in your pockets. At any rate, you have seen plenty of them." The Professor was smiling again. "How many numerals ONE, disregarding the face-plate, series and serial numbers are there on a one-dollar bill?

"The origination of currency in the United States is rather involved, so I won't ask you chaps to tell me when, by an act of the United States Congress (not the Continental Congress) the present currency was established. However, since Congress did establish the present currency the numerals ONE have not been changed on any one-dollar bill!

"You carry or exchange them almost daily. Quickly now! How many numerals ONE are there? I'll give five dollars to the first one with the correct answer. Keep your hands on your desks!"

Without looking, what is your answer? Turn page for solution.

• • CHRISTMAS DINNER FOR THE CLASS • •

Fordney's class was seated at his dinner table. Their beaming faces clearly indicated the affection they felt for him, a feeling that had no connection with the Christmas dinner he had served.

"Here is a note I received in my card from Jack Gildart,

a former student," said the Professor. "It was given to him to mail to me."

Dear Professor Fordney:

No doubt you read in the newspapers two weeks ago of the event that caused my arrest. I am appealing to you because I know you will be quick to appreciate the injustice of my situation. In the first place, I am confident you will believe that I shot King Morrison in self-defense and in protection of my property, which surely is a fundamental right!

When I surprised him robbing my melon patch he became excited and unintentionally, I believe, shot at me. When he refused to put down his gun I fired, and if he hadn't suddenly jumped to the right, the wound would not have been fatal.

Some people in the community believe that I murdered King in cold blood. However, I am sure you will agree

---

Solution — Artless Death

Had Buton fallen from the ladder, his body would not have been where Fordney found it—between where the ladder stood and the house. Motive—Arvonne was Buton's heir.

FOR NEVER, NEVER WICKED MAN WAS WISE — *Pope*

Solution — Class Day

There are nine numerals ONE on a dollar bill! Don't feel bad if you had to look. Several bank tellers didn't know!

THE ALMIGHTY DOLLAR! — *Washington Irving*

that I acted in self-defense. May I count on your help?
                                    Sincerely,
                            LEE MASON, *Durand, Wisconsin.*

"You have fifteen minutes before Mary clears the table for dessert. When it arrives I want you to tell me what you think of the note."

"I'm too full to pay any more attention to it than you did, Professor!" laughed Howard Bell.

What did you find wrong with it? Turn page for solution.

· · INCIDENT OF THE FOUR BOOSTERS · ·

"Remember that gang of female boosters—shoplifters—I've been after for some time?" asked young, alert, attractive policewoman Molly O'Brien. In a deep chair at the other side of his blazing fireplace, Professor Fordney nodded. Molly continued:

"Well, I've got the mob on ice but I can't seem to sort them out. Will you give me a lift, Prof?"

"Certainly, my dear."

"The four girls comprising this gang," Molly went on, "are Myrna Sarni, Dixie Call, Peggy Lomax and Kate Nash. Here are facts concerning them:

"1. The mob leader personally trained the actual booster and the lookout. The fourth girl acts as standby for both.

2. About ten days ago the booster persuaded the leader to take Peggy Lomax into the gang. Peggy used to be a creep joint dancer.

3. The girl who heads the mob is extremely cagey. After she cases a place she always phones the plan of opera-

tion to Myrna Sarni and Myrna passes the details along to the lookout. The lookout then must report back the plan letter-perfect to the leader.

4. Kate Nash and the leader are left-handed.
5. Last week Peggy Lomax saw the booster and the lookout roll a lush of $800. This Peggy reported to the leader who insisted the money be divided four ways.

"And that," concluded Molly O'Brien, "is what I know. What I don't know, Professor, is—who is the mob leader, the actual booster and who is the lookout. Any ideas?"

Fordney chuckled and handed her a note pad on which the answers to her questions were written.

Who is the leader? The booster? The lookout? Turn page for solution.

• • •   A BEAD ON THE BARTENDER   • • •

While only a single bullet had ripped through the dead man's head, there were three bullet holes in the blood-stained wall a few inches above the baseboard.

One shot had been fired from the revolver near Ed Madden's hand.

"Who's the stiff, and what happened?" Inspector Kelley demanded.

"He's Ed Madden, an ex-pug," replied tavern owner Tex Ferrel. "He came in here about 11 o'clock and pro-

---

Solution — Christmas Dinner for the Class

Melons growing in Wisconsin in December!

SEASONS FLOWER AND FADE — Tennyson

---

ceeded to get drunk. I wouldn't serve him anything after 12 o'clock but he had a bottle on him. He said somebody was calling for him at 1:15. I knew he was a bad actor so I left him alone. Everyone else had gone and I thought he was asleep. I was behind the bar when I glanced in the mirror and saw him standing against the wall, a chair in front of him, drawin' a bead on me. He fired as I reached for my gun. I wheeled and shot three times—the last shot dropped him. Nope, ain't touched a thing."

The Professor, who had overheard Ferrel, righted the overturned chair near the 6'3" Madden, went round the bar and stood at the cash register. In a mirror to the left was a bullet hole.

"Where did you keep your gun?" he asked.

"On a shelf to the right of the register."

The criminologist examined Ferrel's automatic from which three shots had been fired. He pointed in the direction of the righted chair.

Kelley nodded. "Self-defense, eh? You deliberately murdered that drunk, Ferrel! Get going."

How did Fordney and Kelley know Ferrel's account was a lie; that he deliberately murdered Madden? Turn page for solution.

How did Fordney and Kelley know Ferrel's account was a lie; that he deliberately murdered Madden? Turn page for solution.

• • • •   EDUCATION FOR DEATH   • • • •

"For a guy with education you certainly miss a lot of answers. What's the trouble now, honey? Better tell mama —she'll unjam you like she has before."

"Shut up! And get out!" Floyd Dexter snapped. "Luigi Marinelli is coming over—that's all."

43

Solution — A Bead on the Bartender

The bullet that passed through Madden's head (and two other bullets) made holes in the wall a few inches above the baseboard, though Ferrel said the 6'3" Madden was standing at the time! This is how they knew, as Ferrel later confessed, that Madden must have been sitting, or sprawled on the floor, when shot. Madden, who had come to blackmail Ferrel, fell out of his chair drunk and Ferrel deliberately shot him as he slouched against the wall. He then fired Madden's gun to authenticate his story.

A LIE HAS NO LEGS AND CANNOT STAND — Warburton

"All right—I'll breeze—but I'm comin' back! You ain't turning the fan on little Mame." The pretty girl flounced from the apartment.

* * *

As the Professor rose from examining Floyd Dexter's body, lying below a wall mirror, a powder-marked hole

Solution — Incident of the Four Boosters

Peggy Lomax (5) is not the booster, lookout or leader.

Myrna Sarni (3) is neither leader nor lookout.

Kate Nash (4) is not the leader.

Therefore, as neither Peggy Lomax, Myrna Sarni nor Kate Nash is the leader, Dixie Call is the leader. The leader, Dixie, is not the lookout or booster. Hence, since neither Dixie Call, Myrna Sarni nor Peggy Lomax is the lookout, Kate Nash occupies that position. So, as Lomax, Call or Nash is not the booster, Myrna Sarni does the actual shoplifting.

44

in the left temple, Inspector Kelley pointed to a newspaper on a table. Fordney read the headlines:

MILLIONAIRE PLAYBOY SHOT LEAVING
THEATER AFTER MATINEE

"Wonder if there's any tie-up with this rompin' Rollo?" Kelley popped a jujube into his mouth. "Let's have it, you!" It was 7:22 P.M.

"I left Floyd's apartment here at 1:30 this afternoon when he said Luigi Marinelli was coming. I returned at 7 and found him dead. No,—didn't touch a thing." Mame's voice broke. "The poor sap just didn't understand that they play for keeps in this town."

* * *

"Sure, my fingerprints are on that newspaper. I took it to Dexter's apartment when I went to collect a little nightclub bill he owed me, this afternoon. Here,"—Marinelli held out a check dated that day for $115.

"What time did you leave?" Fordney asked, examining the check.

"At 3:30. Why?"

The Professor looked at Mame; Kelley stared at the .32 caliber automatic found near the body. A chair scraped. The killer screamed.

Who was arrested for Dexter's murder? What single clue proved guilt? Turn page for solution.

* * *

Professor Fordney found only dust and dried leaves on the winding stairs that led to the top of the abandoned observation tower. He pushed open the unbolted door to the balcony, and stepped out. One hundred and fifty feet below Sheriff Hamilton was kneeling beside the broken body of a man. Completing the circuit of the balcony Fordney hurriedly descended, sniffing the musty air that permeated the tower.

"Just sheer luck we found him in this isolated spot," Hamilton remarked as the Professor joined him. "Few come here this time of year. He hasn't been there long . . . the ground under him is soaked."

From the appearance of his mud-covered shoes it was apparent the man had walked some distance. There were no labels in his well-tailored clothes, and his pockets were empty.

"Your first job, Sheriff, will be to identify him," remarked Fordney, finishing his search. "You'll notice his overcoat, on the back, isn't very wet."

"So I see. Wonder how he knew about the old tower;

Solution — Education for Death

Luigi, who admitted taking the newspaper to Dexter's apartment, said he left at 3:30. This is what trapped him. A paper printed before 3:30 could not possibly have carried an account of the playboy's murder after a matinee performance which would not have finished until considerably later than 3:30!

THUS THE WHIRLIGIG OF TIME BRINGS IN HIS REVENGES — Shakespeare

he's a stranger in these parts. Well, he came to the right spot. It's the only thing high enough around here to jump from and be sure to do a good job."

"You have drawn a natural inference, Sheriff, but he didn't commit suicide," said Fordney, again turning the body over on its face.

How did he know? Turn page for solution.

• FORDNEY HELPS SERGEANT REYNOLDS •

Sergeant Reynolds was baffled. He was sure that the detained Nellie Franklin knew more about the murder of her sweetheart than she had admitted.

She told him that, being entirely deaf in the left ear, she had not heard the sound of the falling body of Barney Eyster, though they were in the same room. Miss Franklin said she had been writing a letter while Barney was standing about fifteen feet to her left, looking out the window. When she turned to ask him a question she saw him on the floor, blood streaming from his head. She attributed the fact that she heard no sound to the probability that a gun with a silencer on it had been fired through the window. "Yes," she said, "I can hear with my right ear as well as anyone."

So strong was Reynolds' hunch he went to seek advice of Professor Fordney who greeted him cordially.

"What brings you here at such an hour?" the latter asked.

"Just a hunch, Prof." Reynolds explained the case.

Fordney listened attentively, then said: "Well, a hunch is just as likely to be right as wrong. However, it is quite a simple matter to tell whether or not Nellie is telling the truth about her deafness." After a pause he continued:

"I'll come with you and we'll whisper simultaneously into her ears two different sentences of the same length. If she cannot repeat either of our sentences we'll know she's not deaf in the left ear."

Reynolds looked bewildered.

What did the Professor mean? Turn page for solution.

• • INCIDENT OF THE TALKING CORPSE • •

When, three days after the raging blizzard ended, neither of the two mysterious and silent men who lived in a small shack at the foot of towering Mount Finger, had put in an appearance at the tiny village of Elmo, Professor Fordney headed a rescue party. Fighting its way through huge drifts, it arrived at the shack at dusk.

On a rough bunk lay the body of a man with his head blown to pieces. He had been dead for at least a week.

Nothing was known of the shack's two occupants, who infrequently called for mail at Elmo, but their names— Ed Morely and Tom Neal. Discouraging all attempts at friendliness they had threatened to shoot anyone who intruded on their solitude.

A torn half of a letter signed "McGee" was in the dead

Solution — The Abandoned Tower

As Fordney found only dust and dried leaves on the tower steps he knew the dead man had not walked up them. If he had, his muddy shoes would have left tracks.

WHY? HERE'S A VILLAIN? ABLE TO CORRUPT A THOUSAND BY EXAMPLE — Massinger

man's pocket, identifying him as one of McGee's gang. McGee had broken prison and was the object of an intense police search. The Professor knew also that every member of McGee's gang knew their leader had been framed by a rival mob member and all had openly threatened to knock off McGee's betrayer.

The only other information Fordney could discover concerning the two was contained in torn bits of paper which, when pasted together, disclosed that Neal and Morely had quarrelled when, through accident, Morely discovered that Neal was the man who had framed McGee.

"Now we got a killer to find," drawled Sheriff Egen. "If we only knew who this leader is, we'd know which one to look for, but . . .

"The corpse," said Fordney, "is . . . so go out and bring in . . ."

Who was the dead man? How do you know? Turn page for solution.

• • **DAMON IN THE DRAMA OF DEATH** • •

"A flickering light, through the partly opened door of Nona's room, made grotesque arabesques in the darkened corridor as I hurried past," explained Carlisle Damon, once-famous actor.

"Never mind being poetic," retorted Inspector Kelley. "Get on with the facts."

Professor Fordney smiled at his friend's impatience. The three men were discussing the tragedy that had occurred in the cheap boarding house a few doors from the actor's room.

Nothing had been touched, so Damon declared, until the arrival of Kelley and Fordney who saw, in the dim rays of a small electric lamp standing on a night table, the body of Nona Nason lying across the bed, a knife in her heart. The door offered the only means of escape from the room. The girl's hand, clutching the dagger, pointed to suicide.

"I had just passed her door when I heard a groan, hollow and sepulchral," continued Damon. "I turned. Those

---

Solution — Fordney Helps Sergeant Reynolds

If a person pretends to be deaf in one ear the truth can be discovered with certainty by two persons simultaneously whispering different words in the two ears. If one ear is quite deaf the person can naturally understand what is whispered in the other ear and can repeat it. But if the person can hear with both ears what is whispered, he cannot repeat the conversations. Try it on your friends!

PRETENSION ALMOST ALWAYS OVERDOES THE ORIGINAL AND HENCE EXPOSES ITSELF — Ballou

---

Solution — Incident of the Talking Corpse

The letter in the dead man's pocket identified him as a member of McGee's gang. As McGee had been framed by a rival gang member, and as Morely discovered Neal was the man who had framed his leader, obviously the dead man was Morely.

I WILL KILL THEE A HUNDRED AND FIFTY WAYS — Shakespeare

flickering shadows seemed a portent of death! Then a long shuddering sigh! Cold sweat stood on my forehead but I squared my shoulders and entered. She was dead! Poor girl! I suppose she found the battle too tough and . . ."

"Never mind the dramatics! You're not on the stage now!" interrupted Kelley. "You're quite sure no one left her room?"

"I'd swear to that."

"Cut it out," bellowed Kelley. "Either someone did leave her room, you've made an inaccurate statement, or you're involved in the murder!"

Why did Kelley make this statement? Turn page for solution.

• • • • • •   CASE #194   • • • • • •

Rudolph Mayer stumbled into the police station of the little village of Monroe, shook water from his clothes, and collapsed. A local physician was summoned and brought Mayer around. He told the following story.

"My wife and I, fond of winter sports, registered at the Fox Head Resort this afternoon—I've spent several vacations here. Shortly before dusk we decided to go skating on Lake Howard. We'd been out probably twenty minutes, as nearly as I can figure it, when my wife, who was about ten yards in front of me, suddenly dropped into the water through a large hole. Someone must have been cutting ice. I swerved, took off my skates, and jumped in after her. Despite my efforts, however, I couldn't locate her. I was barely able to pull myself out, and as I called and there was no help at hand, made my way here, somehow. It's about half a mile, I guess, and I didn't think

I'd be able to do it. For God's sake send someone out there!"

Again the man fainted but was revived in a few minutes, mumbling incoherently about skates.

Two constables were dispatched through the ten below zero weather to the scene and returned with Mayer's skates found on the edge of a large hole where a local concern had been cutting ice. At the sight of them Mayer again collapsed.

* * *

Professor Fordney read no further in the above newspaper account.

"Mayer is certainly lying," he said to himself.

How did he know? Turn page for solution.

• • • • THE PROFESSOR ACCUSED • • • •

On the second day of his vacation at the Blue Cow Inn, in Yorkshire, England, Professor Fordney learned from the proprietor that an old acquaintance lived nearby. Receiving directions, he set off for an early morning call.

Knocks at both the front and back doors brought no response. He was about to leave when Mrs. Halstead, the

<hr>

Solution — Damon in the Drama of Death

As the girl's room was lighted by a small electric lamp, Damon could not have seen the flickering shadows he twice mentioned.

NO, NO, I AM BUT A SHADOW OF MYSELF; YOU ARE DECEIVED, MY SUBSTANCE IS NOT HERE — *Shakespeare*

housekeeper, approached the cottage. Introducing himself with difficulty, since Mrs. Halstead seemed to have trouble hearing, he stated that possibly something was wrong. After unlocking the front door with a key produced from a voluminous pocket, she went upstairs to her employer's bedroom while he pushed open a door on the ground floor and found George Docker dead. He gently closed it; silently moved about searching for possible clues.

* * *

"Did you disturb anything on finding Mr. Docker dead?" apologetically asked Coroner Hittingdon. He knew the criminologist's reputation.

"I merely locked the library door—the key was in it—to make sure . . ." answered Professor Fordney.

"That ain't true, Your Honor," interrupted Mrs. Halstead. "As I came downstairs this man was movin' about in the room, then he came out, locked the door and wouldn't let me in. Said he must summon the police! Bah! He did the marster in all right!"

The coroner shouted several questions at her, and her repeated inquiries, "What?", irritated him.

"I may be deaf but I ain't dumb!" the redoubtable housekeeper said. "He killed the marster . . . and him callin' himself a detective!"

Fordney smiled. "Mr. Coroner, you'd better insist she tell the truth!"

What did he mean? Turn page for solution.

"Some years ago Morrofsky, in person, combined with George Arliss in the film "House of Rothschild," had packed the Paramount. Every seat was occupied and standing room was at a premium. What a premiere it was!" The Professor was relating a ten-year-old incident to his class.

"As the picture neared its end and the orchestra, under Morrofsky's magnificent leadership, reached the climax of Mascagni's 'Cavalleria Rusticana,' a shot rang out.

Solution — Case # 194

If the newspaper account was correct Mayer was lying. He could not possibly have been in the water, walked half a mile through ten below zero weather, and then shaken water from his clothes. Had the tragedy happened as he described it, the water on his clothes would have been frozen.

WINTER DOES NOT WORK ONLY ON A BROAD SCALE; HE IS CAREFUL OF TRIFLES — Smith

Solution — The Professor Accused

Mrs. Halstead admitted she was deaf, yet she stated Professor Fordney was moving about in the room, the door to which was closed, as she came down the stairs. Had she been deaf she could not possibly have heard Fordney investigating the library. She was later convicted of the murder of her employer.

WE ARE ONLY VULNERABLE AND RIDICULOUS THROUGH OUR PRETENSIONS — Mme. de Girardin

"Inspector Kelley, who accompanied me, was immediately on his feet bellowing, 'Lights!' They were quickly turned on and the picture stopped. Warning everyone to keep his place, we started for the back of the theatre when a man's body slumped out of a seat and fell almost at our feet. A hurried examination disclosed he had been shot in the back of the head and that he was an extremely tall man.

"Leaving Kelley to look after things, I hurried to the operator's booth. When almost there I heard another shot and I knew I was too late. Entering the small compartment hung under the balcony I found the operator with a bullet through his temple and a smoking revolver by his side.

"Not much to this," I remarked as Kelley joined me.

"'I wonder if he got the right man?' commented the Inspector.

"'I don't understand how he could have made such a splendid shot under the circumstances. Amazing!'"

"Was the dead man sitting in an aisle seat?" interrupted one of the class.

"Yes," replied Fordney.

"Baloney!" was the inelegant comment. "I've already spotted the flaw in that yarn, Prof!"

Did you? What is it? Turn page for solution.

"Well, Joe, how are all the dear little Rollos out at the University?" Inspector Kelley asked, filling his glass from the Professor's decanter and sinking into a huge chair before the cheery fire.

Fordney chuckled. Three of the Inspector's best men were graduates of his class in criminology.

"Here," he replied, "is a copy of a report from an ex-Rollo, Jack Hurley, now a rookie with the Boston Bureau. See what you make of it."

Kelley snorted as he read:

The four members of this dope gang are Elsie Byrd, Bat Harmon, Gil Tolden and Maxine Jarsoca. One of them was recently released from prison. Two are Americans; two foreigners.

1. Three days ago the gang leader heard Maxine Jarsoca and the ring's front discussing split in profits.
2. The leader told Elsie Byrd he had fallen hard for Maxine's sister.
3. Tolden and the gang front, and the member just out of prison were recently in an automobile accident.

Solution — Class Day

The student readily recognized the absurdity of the Professor's story which he had given to his class to test their quick detection of a glaring inconsistency. An orchestra under personal leadership does not play during the showing of talking motion pictures!

WIT MARRIES IDEAS LYING FAR APART, BY A SUDDEN JERK OF THE UNDERSTANDING — *Whipple*

4. We arrested Maxine and her ring sweetheart in the gang's hideout. We got the other two as they boarded an eastbound train.

5. Another interesting fact is that the leader, the front, and Bat Harmon are all blond.

"This," bellowed Kelley, "is the damnedest bucketful of bellywash I've ever seen! I'd break any man who wrote such farrago. Well—don't sit there like a blinkin' billiken. Who is the leader of this diluted dope ring that any good dick could have rounded up between roll calls?"

The Professor laughed heartily as he informed his friend.

Who is the leader; who is the front? Turn page for solution.

• • • • • **A LIE GETS THE AX** • • • • •

"The body's under the wood pile, but remember—you gotta keep me outa this," whined Stig Carona, casting shifty eyes at Professor Fordney and Inspector Kelley. Sniffing through a nose which an ungenerous nature had placed at an unlovely angle and licking lips cut on the bias, Stig twisted his greasy cap in nervous fingers.

An hour later the three men got out of a police car and walked to a clump of bushes in Wilson's woods.

"Bill and Jake were fightin' in front of that shack over there," Stig explained, pointing to a clearing. "Jake knocked Bill down, then grabbed an ax. When Bill got up Jake hit him over the head with it a couple of times. Then he dragged the body toward the shack. He must've thought he heard somethin' 'cause he propped it up against the house and walked over this way. I knew if he found

57

me here I'd get what Bill got, so I lammed to the road, jumped in my car and went for the cops."

Fordney observed bloodstains on the shack about three feet from the ground which appeared to bear out Stig's story. Some freshly cut fire wood spattered with dark stains lay near a chopping block.

Opening the door of the shack the Professor was about to enter when Kelley called from the yard. "The body's under the wood pile, all right. Gad, what a sight!"

But Fordney's interest at the moment was not the body but a bright, clean, shining ax standing in the far corner of the shack's single room. Carrying it by its battered handle, he took it outside. At the Professor's quiet words Stig turned with a startled look.

"Unless," said Fordney, "you want to be placed under arrest for murder immediately, you will tell us the truth about this crime."

How did Fordney know Stig's account was untrue? Turn page for solution.

How did Fordney know Stig's account was untrue? Turn page for solution.

Solution — Help Yourself

1. Maxine Jarsoca is neither leader nor front.
2. Elsie Byrd is not the leader.
3. Tolden is not the front.
4. Bat Harmon is neither leader nor front. Hence Gil Tolden is the leader, Elsie Byrd the front.

Twenty minutes after Mr. Stanton reported that Burg, his private watchman, had scared off a prowler, Professor Fordney was examining that part of the six-foot stone wall surrounding the millionaire's suburban estate where Burg said the man had shinnied up and dropped over. Freshly made marks were apparent.

Calling for a ladder, he climbed to the top and after several minutes' examination dropped heavily to the new and as yet unopened concrete road. He walked fifty yards to the north and south hoping to find some clue, some indication to confirm the watchman's story. Finding none, he returned to the house where he talked with Stanton; he said he had received two threatening letters and, while he had not informed the authorities, he had employed a private watchman.

* * *

"I've found this out about the Stanton affair," Inspector Kelley told Fordney next day. "Some of my stool pigeons learned through the underworld grapevine that Jack McCawley did prowl the Stanton estate yesterday, that when scared off by a watchman he climbed the wall, broke his nose when he fell to the road, and escaped in a car he had hidden in a lane a hundred yards away. I've had all his usual haunts covered, but haven't yet been able to find him. At that," Kelley continued, taking a deep breath, "I think this time we've done more at this end than you have. What do you know about the case?"

"Not much, except that either your stool pigeons or Stanton's watchman is lying," replied Fordney.

Why did Fordney think so? Turn page for solution.

A multitude of small accidents had delayed Ruth Mundy. The battery in her car had gone dead and she had to call a cab; she had mislaid the key to the strong box! Just as the taxi pulled up she located it. Hastily snatching from the dresser drawer two twenty-dollar bills, one old and crumpled, one crisp and new, she thrust them loosely into her bag. In her hurry, the perfume bottle on the dresser upset, spilling perfume on her lovely moire purse! If this kept up she'd be late for her birthday party! Now, where was that book she was to return? She was

---

Solution — A Lie Gets the Ax

Had Stig's account been true he could not possibly have known where the body was. By his own admission he last saw it propped up against the house.

MEN'S MINDS ARE TOO INGENIOUS IN PALLIATING GUILT IN THEMSELVES — Livy

---

Solution — The Underworld Grapevine

Fordney knew of course that had McCawley broken his nose when falling on the concrete road he would have bled profusely; yet he found no clue that McCawley had fallen to the road.

BLOOD FOLLOWS BLOOD — Defoe

sure she had just put it on the dresser! Finally locating it under her coat on the bed, she grabbed it and ran.

Once in the taxi she opened her bag and fumbled for her vanity case. Its clasp opened and she stuck her finger in the paste rouge. Another casualty! Well, it didn't get on anything else, that was one break. Removing all traces of the rouge with her handkerchief, she threw it away.

Arriving at the Mayflower Hotel she handed the driver a bill. While she waited for her change Professor Fordney alighted from his car and greeted her with a "Hello, Ruth."

Acknowledging the greeting she turned to the driver. "You've made a mistake. This is change for five. I gave you a twenty."

"Oh no, lady! You gave me five dollars!"

Fordney listened amused while Ruth excitedly proved she'd given the driver a twenty-dollar bill.

"How's that, Professor?" she laughed.

How did Ruth prove her story? Turn page for solution.

• • • • • • • • **ALIBI** • • • • • • • •

The Professor was in an expansive mood.

"I've often observed," he told his dinner guests, "how extremely difficult it is to fake an unassisted alibi. The recent Werner affair in Chicago is a case in point." He fired a cigar and continued:

"I had no suspicion of Werner when I bumped into him on Michigan Avenue the morning after a friend of his had been found murdered. When I casually inquired where he'd been between 4 and 6 o'clock the previous afternoon, he gave the following account.

" 'It was such a glorious afternoon that about 2 o'clock

61

I went for a sail. When I was about eight miles off shore —about 5:30—the wind died down completely. There wasn't a breath of air. Drifting about I recalled that the International distress signal is a flag flown upside down, so I ran mine to the top of the mast in that manner and waited in the dead calm.

" 'Shortly after 6 o'clock the freighter *Luella* hove to and I went aboard her after securing my boat with a towline. Her skipper said he'd seen my distress signal about three miles away. He put me ashore at Harvey's Landing and a passing car gave me a lift to town. Imagine my surprise when I read in the morning paper that the *Luella* had sunk in a storm last night and all hands had been lost!' "

The Professor sipped his wine and went on:

"While the *Luella* had been sunk with loss of entire crew, I immediately arrested Werner for further questioning. I knew his alibi was faked."

How did the Professor know? Turn page for solution.

How did the Professor know? Turn page for solution.

Solution — Ruth's Birthday

Very simple. Her bill smelled of the perfume she'd spilled on her purse.

AND WHEN A LADY'S IN THE CASE, YOU KNOW ALL OTHER THINGS GIVE PLACE — *Gay*

Handsome Willie Montford whistled a gay tune as he adjusted his tie in the mirror. Behind him his apartment door opened silently. Willie froze in fear and panic. In the glass he saw a girl. She had a gun in her hand. The girl fired. Handsome Willie Montford pitched to the floor, dead.

* * *

"I'm probably Willie's best friend," Joe Gulino told Professor Fordney, "but Willie was the most close-mouthed guy I ever saw so I don't know much about him. He lived off of women—but I suppose you know that. All I know is that he had three underworld dames on the string: Dottie Kinble, Elsie Drake and Connie Laird. He was playing them against each other. When I told him it was dangerous he just laughed and said he could handle them. Looks like one of them handled him."

* * *

Fordney and Lieutenant Bill Jopke went to work in the underworld. They discovered that one of the girls and Willie Montford ran a cheap bookie joint. Also that Elsie Drake only recently had learned about the place, and told Montford his partner was a dope addict.

Further investigation revealed the following:

1. Connie Laird's husband was the brother of the man who was married to the woman who killed Montford.

2. The beautiful girl who ran the bookie joint with Montford had never been married. While she spurned all offers she had begged Montford to marry her.

It wasn't much, but the criminologist sorted out the information and knew which of the three women had shot Handsome Willie Montford.

Do you? Turn page for solution.

Do you? Turn page for solution.

• • • • **THE EX-WIFE MURDER** • • • •

"Who shot her?" cried Rogers as he rushed into the hospital three minutes after his ex-wife died from a bullet through her head.

"Just a minute," Professor Fordney said. "I'd like to ask you a few questions . . . routine, you know. Although divorced for the past six months, you have been living in the same house with your ex-wife, have you not?"

"That's right."

"Had any trouble recently?"

"Well . . . yesterday when I told her I was going on a business trip, she threatened suicide. In fact, I grabbed a bottle of iodine from her as she was about to drink it. When I left last evening at seven, however, telling her I

Solution — Alibi

In a dead calm Werner's flag would have hung limp against the mast and the *Luella's* captain could not possibly have seen at such distance whether or not it was upside down. There was another, though minor, flaw in Werner's account. While the International distress signal is a flag flown upside down, it is by custom and regulation flown at half-mast.

HOW HAPPY HE WHO CAN STILL HOPE TO LIFT HIMSELF FROM THIS SEA OF ERROR — Goethe

was spending the night with friends in Sewickley, she made no objections. Returning to town this afternoon," he continued, "I called my home and the maid answered."

"Just what did she say?"

" 'Oh, Mr. Rogers, they took poor mistress to St. Anne's hospital 'bout half an hour ago. Please hurry to her!' She was crying so I couldn't get anything else out of her; then I hurried here. Where is she?"

"The nurse here will direct you," responded the Professor.

"A queer case this, Joe," said Inspector Kelley who had been listening to the conversation. "These moderns are a little too much for me! A man and woman living together after being divorced six months!"

"A queer case, indeed, Jim," sighed Fordney. "You'd better detain Rogers. If he didn't shoot her himself, I'm confident he knows who did."

Why did the Professor advise the Inspector to detain Rogers? Turn page for solution.

• • • • • • **FATE COMPELS** • • • • • •

Though it had fallen from the second floor to the cellar, the old iron safe landed in almost vertical position. The fire of the previous night had destroyed part of the old house, burning to death miserly old Jonathan Aiken and his dog. Jonathan's grandson, Tom Drewery, arrived home from Philadelphia at 11:30 P.M. just as the fire was brought under control.

The Professor was surprised to find that the small, tidy stacks of loose stamps on the floor had a market value of only about $8,000, for it was generally supposed that the wealthy philatelist's collection was worth at least $125,000.

Aiken's penchant for keeping his most valuable stamps loose and unalbumed also was common knowledge. "Can't get close enough to the little beauties if they're in books," he frequently said.

Drewery showed that solemnity and restraint befitting the circumstances as he answered Fordney's questions. That tramp had done a thorough job and would never

---

Solution — The Pay-off

Willie Montford's bookie joint partner was not Elsie Drake. Therefore this girl was either Dottie Kinble or Connie Laird. Connie Laird and the killer both were married and as Montford's partner was not married, it was Dottie Kinble who ran the bookie joint with Montford. Hence, as Montford's murderer and Connie Laird were married, and neither Connie nor Dottie Kinble (who was single) was the killer, it was Elsie Drake who murdered Handsome Willie Montford.

THAT CRAWLING INSECT, WHO FROM MUD BEGAN, WARMED BY MY BEAMS, AND KINDLED INTO MAN! — Dryden

---

Solution — The Ex-Wife Murder

Rogers could not have known his ex-wife had been shot unless he had guilty knowledge of the crime. The maid did not say why she had been taken to the hospital, yet Rogers' first words on entering it were "Who shot her?"

I THINK THE FIRST WISDOM IS TO RESTRAIN THE TONGUE — Cato

talk. He had the stamps—and the old man's fortune! Fire away!

"Was the safe opened before our arrival?" the Professor asked.

"No," Drewery replied. "It wasn't touched—and it was under my observation all night. I sat up in the living room."

Fordney's eyes took in the young man's meticulous grooming.

Drewery laughed. "Oh, I bathed and changed clothes," he said.

"Quite," murmured the criminologist, noting the man's unshaven face. "For the present you will be charged with robbery. Later no doubt this will be changed to arson and murder!"

A single clue proved the safe had not been robbed after he fire. What was it? Turn page for solution.

AFFAIR OF THE LEFT-HANDED VICTIM •

Professor Fordney removed three shreds of tobacco from he revolver barrel, inserted into it a helixometer and murmured to himself. Swiftly he took the gun apart.

The cylinder contained four .38 caliber cartridges and two empty shells. He observed that it had been fired recently. The gas rings around the chambers holding the empty shells held his interest. Otherwise the revolver was clean . . . extremely clean.

"I wonder now," he mused.

Tom Gilmore, bit actor in Westerns, had been killed at 9 P.M. in the beach cabin of motion picture star Warren Warwick. The only witness other than Warwick was picture starlet Anita Duval who had been secretly married to

Gilmore for a year, though they lived apart. Anita said she had gone to Warwick's to discuss her role in a forthcoming production. An hour later, Gilmore, who was drunk, forced his way in, whipped a revolver from his pocket (the one Fordney was examining) and without a word fired twice at Warwick, the bullets entering the wall behind the actor's head. As Gilmore was about to fire the third time Warwick shot in self-defense, immediately notified the police.

This completely corroborated Warwick's version of the tragedy. Nothing, he said, had been touched before arrival of the police.

Bullets from the wall and both guns had been carefully handled and wrapped by the police and dispatched to Fordney with a note advising that Gilmore was left-handed and minus the left little finger.

Examination revealing that bullets taken from Warwick's wall had been fired from Gilmore's gun, the criminologist recommended detention of Warwick and Anita. Both were lying.

How did Fordney know? Turn page for solution.

Solution — Fate Compels

Having fallen through two floors, the Professor knew, the stamps would have been scattered about the safe floor, not piled in "tidy stacks" as he found them. Unthinkingly Drewery arranged the stamps he left after taking the most valuable in the familiar small piles of Aiken's custom.

THE COMPULSION OF FATE IS BITTER — Wieland

"After I opened the eyes of the fish lying on the river bank it gave a gasp and died, so I knew that someone probably had been in the vicinity shortly before," Fordney told his class in criminology.

"There were too many overlapping footprints to enable me to distinguish whether or not my suspect was one of those who had been walking there recently. I examined the fish more closely and found it had not been caught with a hook. That also gave me food for thought," he continued.

"With the aid of the police I succeeded in locating Bill Johnson whom from the first I suspected of the murder of May Turner. Her mutilated body had been found on the river bank by a farmer living nearby. My interrogation of Johnson was rather unsuccessful. He was a big, burly, sullen creature who refused to answer my questions concerning the murder. I don't believe in the third degree, as you know, so I left Johnson alone and questioned the farmer.

"Now, while I don't want you young chaps to take anything for granted, experience does bring a certain psychic sense regarding the reliability of a witness, so when the farmer told me he knew nothing of the tragedy, I believed him. Then . . ."

"You haven't told us this farmer's name," Jim Boyle rather gruffly interjected.

"What difference does that make?" the Professor inquired.

"Why it doesn't make any!" excitedly exclaimed Harry Simmons, a newcomer to the class. "Can't you fellows see what's wrong with the Professor's story? I can!"

Can you? Turn page for solution.

"Listen, you guys!" The man's voice was excited. He read from an old history of the Pinkertons. "What a gag! What a gag! This suitcase dodge is so old it's new. Let's give it a workout!"

"Sounds kosher to me," agreed Bulgy Eyes.

"It stinks!" was Dead Pan's subtle comment.

"We'll try it," announced Two Quart.

* * *

Solution — Affair of the Left-Handed Victim

Warwick said nothing had been touched until the police arrived. Both guns were "carefully wrapped and handled" by the police, yet Fordney found tobacco in Gilmore's gun barrel! As a fired bullet cleans the barrel of everything but traces of its own passage, the Professor knew Anita and Warwick were lying about the affair. Warwick was convicted of manslaughter; Anita acquitted.

FALSEHOOD AVAILS ITSELF OF HASTE AND UNCERTAINTY — Tacitus

Solution — Class Day

No fish can close its eyes! Another test the Professor gave his class on observation of the commonplace.

O SCALY, SLIPPERY, WET, SWIFT, STARING WEIGHTS WHAT IS'T YE DO? WHAT LIFE LEAD? EH, DULL GOGGLES? — Hunt

Cattleman Jim Bragan braked his car to a sharp stop. He couldn't leave a new piece of luggage lying in the road! He got out, walked back.

An hour later another motorist found him unconscious in a ditch, robbed of $1800.

On information supplied Sheriff Waters by tourist camp operator Tad Moran, one of whose cabins housed five suspicious men, the following were arrested: Al Munson, Fred Taggert, Skip Crocker, Monk Ward, Joe Hudson.

From Moran and several of the neighbors, Waters and Professor Fordney gleaned some interesting information.

1. One of the above five men rented the cabin for the gang after arguing with Crocker and Taggert, who were strictly from the city.
2. It was the pal of the cabin renter who read of the suitcase dodge. After some discussion, these two persuaded the two bandits, who robbed Bragan, to try it.
3. Hudson advised the bandits against it.
4. Munson loaned the two robbers his suitcase and the man who rented the cabin gave them his car for the job.

The sheriff put down his Christmas pencil and scratched his elbow. "Makes a nice little game doesn't it, Prof?" he observed. "But who wins?"

"I can tell you which two lose," chuckled Fordney.

Who were the two bandits? Turn page for solution.

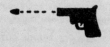

During a lull in the storm which tossed and rocked the sturdy little steamer *Dauntless,* a shot rang out on A deck.

Professor Fordney threw down the detective story he was somewhat unsuccessfully trying to read and hastened into the companionway. Where it turned at the far corner, he found Steward Mierson bending over the body of a man who had been instantly killed. Just then the heavens opened; lightning flashed and thunder boomed as if in ghoulish mockery.

The dead man's head bore powder burns. Captain Larson and the criminologist started checking the whereabouts of everyone aboard, beginning with those passengers nearest where the body was discovered.

The first questioned was Nathan Cohen, who said he

Solution — So Old It's New

(1) Neither Crocker nor Taggert rented the cabin.

(2) The man who read of the suitcase trick did not rent the cabin, and neither he nor the renter is one of the bandits.

(3) Hudson did not rent the cabin or read about the suitcase scheme, nor is he either of the bandits.

(4) Munson is not the cabin renter nor is he a bandit.

Hence Monk Ward rented the cabin, but as he is not one of the bandits (2) the bandits are Taggert and Crocker.

ROGUES ARE ALWAYS FOUND OUT IN SOME WAY — La Fontaine

---

was just completing a letter in his cabin when he heard the shot.

"May I see it?" Larson asked.

Looking over the captain's shoulder Fordney saw the small, precise handwriting, on the ship's stationery. The letter was apparently written to a woman.

The next cabin was occupied by Miss Margaret Millsworth. On being questioned regarding what she was doing at the time, Miss Millsworth became excited and nervous. She stated that she had become so frightened by the storm, that about fifteen minutes before the shot was fired she had gone to the cabin of her fiancé, James Montgomery, directly opposite. The latter corroborated her statement, saying they hadn't rushed into the passageway because it would have looked compromising were they seen emerging together at that hour. Fordney noticed a dark red stain on Montgomery's dressing gown.

The whereabouts of the rest of the passengers and crew were satisfactorily checked.

Whom did the captain hold on suspicion? Why? Turn page for solution.

• • • • **THE PROFESSOR DEDUCES** • • • •

From the open window (outside of which stood a tall ladder) at the end of the long hall, to a settee beneath a portrait of an eighteenth-century Scot in kilts, the set of muddy footprints was easily followed. There they ended.

"Maybe the bra' laddie has 'em hid under yon kilts," Inspector Kelley observed facetiously.

Twenty feet further down the hall, the Professor re-entered the bedroom where Donald McLennan lay in his bed, bludgeoned to death. Signaling Kelley to switch on the lights, he went to his knees. This time his thoroughness was rewarded.

From door to bed and return he observed under his glass a number of faint, incomplete right foot marks. He was confident they were made by a shoeless, tiptoeing person. Nowhere were impressions of a left foot found. A singular puzzling fact was that the prints were of a faint bluish color; the blue a trifle deeper in the center. The Professor explained to Kelley.

"So," the Inspector snorted, "a one-legged pixie playing hopscotch on tiptoe bounces in here, ups with his shillelagh, conks the old gent, does a broken-toe dance, then exits blithely singing, 'Armfuls of Purple!' "

Fordney chuckled as he regarded a dripping sky roofing a soggy world. Examining the muddy ladder he murmured, "Quite . . ."

"Quite what!" bellowed Kelley.

"Why, it's quite evident how those footprints in the murder room were made," answered Fordney. "A few simple deductions give us one negative and two positive clues concerning the killer's dress. You see, Jim, he must have been wearing . . ."

This is a factual problem in deduction exclusively for supersleuths. What deductions did Fordney make from the footprints that enabled him to describe three points of the killer's dress? Turn page for solution.

Turn page for solution.

Solution — Murder on Board

Nathan Cohen was held because it would have been impossible for him to have written in small, precise handwriting during a violent storm.

THE STORM IS UP, AND ALL IS ON THE HAZARD — *Shakespeare*

"Hurry . . . hurry . . . Fordney!" came the agitated voice over the phone. "Waterman speaking. They've got me! You'll . . .!"

As the Professor called "Hello! Hello!" he heard a shot, a thud, and then—silence!

Jumping into his car, he hurried to the Waterman home. As he was about to alight, Morris, the judge's chauffeur, ran over.

"I'm glad you're here, sir," he exclaimed. "The judge has been murdered!"

Entering the library Fordney found Waterman lying dead on the floor, blood from a temple wound staining the rich Oriental rug.

"How did it happen?" he demanded.

"I had just put up the car," said Morris, "and was going across the lawn when I noticed the French doors were open. Knowing the judge was alone in the house, I decided to investigate. As I was about to step into the room I heard him talking to you and saw a masked man standing in the doorway. A second later the man fired and ran. The judge fell from a bullet in the temple and I dashed around the house after the killer. I've been searching the grounds ever since but have found no trace of him. He must have escaped."

"Why didn't you first summon help?"

"Why, I was sure Judge Waterman was dead and I wanted to get his murderer."

"Have you a gun?"

"Yes . . . here it is!"

With only a glance at it Fordney pocketed the revolver, opened the door of the cabinet, removed the phone, and when Inspector Kelley at headquarters answered, said,

"Judge Waterman has just been murdered. I'll hold his chauffeur until you get here. Perhaps I'll get the truth out of him before you arrive."

How did the Professor know Morris was lying? Turn page for solution.

Solution — The Professor Deduces

From the faint, incomplete shoeless right foot impressions in the murder room, the Professor deduced (and correctly) that they were made by a man wearing cheap blue socks, the right one sufficiently wet for the cheap dye to run. As the blue was deeper in the center he reasoned that the man had a hole in his right shoe which accounted for the wetness of the right sock. As there were no impressions of a left foot, Fordney deduced that the left sock had not become wet, therefore, that there was no hole in the left shoe. Although he could not definitely determine the sex of the tiptoeing murderer from the incomplete footprints he was reasonably sure the killer was a man, both from the nature of the crime and the fact that women's blue hose are not common. The killer was caught in less than three hours. He sits in the death house at this moment vainly trying to cover his fear of that last summons.

DISCERNMENT IS A POWER OF THE UNDERSTANDING IN WHICH FEW EXCEL — Oreville

Professor Fordney and Sergeant Reynolds had just arrived from headquarters in response to a telephone call from the house of the eccentric bachelor, Robert Duval.

Duval's sister, greatly agitated, met them at the door. "I'm afraid something terrible has happened," she said. "I came to the house to see Robert ten minutes ago. As soon as I opened the front door I noticed a strong odor of gas. There was no answer to my shouts and I thought I'd better get help. Since phoning you I discovered the gas seems to be coming from the study, but I was afraid to go in."

Unlocking the door, Reynolds met some slight resistance in pushing it open. Pillow stuffing had been jammed along the bottom, and the same stuffing had been used in the cracks of the windows which were securely locked.

Duval lay dead upon the couch, a knotted scarf around his throat. The room was heavy with gas issuing from the fireplace log.

A search revealed a note left by Duval which read, *IF MY DEATH OCCURS UNDER SUSPICIOUS CIRCUMSTANCES ARREST OLSON.*

"Say," exclaimed Reynolds, "this looks bad for Olson! I'd better hunt up that bird!"

"You might talk with him, Sergeant, but you'll see he can't be arrested for this."

Why? Turn page for solution.

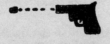

"This is a stick-up!" barked the burly leader of the four masked men as they entered the Third National Bank. "Any of you twitch an eyelid and you'll be cold meat. You

---

Solution — The Murder of Judge Waterman

Morris said the masked intruder shot the judge and ran from the house. Fordney knew Waterman had been killed while phoning him. The chauffeur said he dashed around the house after the murderer and had been searching for him until the Professor arrived.

Had he been telling the truth, the telephone could not have been in the cabinet with the door closed, as Fordney found it.

SOME CIRCUMSTANTIAL EVIDENCE IS VERY STRONG, AS WHEN YOU FIND A TROUT IN THE MILK — Thoreau

---

Solution — A Revengeful Attempt

It was obviously a case of suicide. The door, with stuffing at the bottom on the inside, was locked on the outside. The windows, with cracks stuffed, were also locked. Therefore, no one could possibly have left the room. Duval, with an intense hatred for Olson, had locked the door on the outside, gone around and entered the study through a window, made his preparations, written the note hoping to incriminate his enemy, and killed himself.

REVENGE IS SWEETER THAN LIFE ITSELF. SO THINK FOOLS — Juvenal

there with the gimp, get back of that cage and open the safe or I'll bat your skull open."

The terrified employees obeyed the gang leader's orders and the mob made a safe getaway with $46,000, but not before one of the gang ruthlessly shot and killed the cashier.

Informed of the above, the Professor went into action. He was satisfied the robbery was the work of the Ardmore mob composed of Joe Kreble, Rex Bender, Tony Faracchi and Dick Doran. After tapping every possible underworld source, Fordney was certain of the following:

1. One of the four, an ex-automobile racer, was the getaway driver for the gang.
2. Figuring on a side racket, Rex Bender had tried for a month to get the driver to go in with him on the deal, but the driver was leery. He didn't trust Bender; thought he might be pulling a double cross.
3. The driver and Joe Kreble recently had won heavily from Dick Doran in a crap game run by the uncle of one of the mob.
4. The killer of the cashier and the driver are very close friends.
5. On a recent stock market tip Doran netted $9,000 which he split with the man who murdered the cashier as the latter put up the money.

The Professor pressed his buzzer. Sergeant Bill Jopke entered.

"Go out and bring in . . . . dead or alive!" snapped Fordney.

Who killed the bank cashier? Turn page for solution.

* * *

Phew! He'd almost slipped there. It just wasn't in character. And that . . . What was the matter with him? A drink was what he needed.

* * *

"Rowel's prints are on this glass and over those of the girl's on the empty cocktail shaker," Sergeant Aden said. "But while Manfield's prints are on this other glass they are not on . . ."

"I can't help how it looks—or sounds," Rex Manfield interrupted, "but it's the truth, Professor. Lil dropped in about 3 o'clock. At 3:15 Walter here came down—his apartment is two floors above. He shook up a cocktail. We had a drink and he left. A few minutes later I received a phone call to report immediately for an emergency air raid warden meeting. I left Lil here. At headquarters I learned the call was a hoax. When I returned, Lil was strangled to death!"

"How many drinks did you and Lil have?" Fordney asked.

"Just the one Walter poured us," Manfield replied. "The shaker is practically empty."

Solution — The Killer

The getaway driver is not Rex Bender (2), Joe Kreble or Dick Doran (3), therefore the driver is Tony Faracchi. The driver (Faracchi) is not the murderer (4). Rex Bender is not the killer (2 & 4). Dick Doran (5) is not the murderer, hence the man who shot the bank cashier is Joe Kreble.

"Then Lil finished it after I left. One drink never did satisfy her."

"What about that . . ." The Professor pointed.

"I . . . I . . . don't know," answered Manfield. "Somebody must have . . . but why should they?"

"I don't suppose, Rowel, you returned here after you left?" said Fordney.

"No. I didn't know Rex had gone out."

"How is it, Mr. Manfield, that you didn't inform Rowel of the tragedy immediately after calling the police?"

"Too upset, I guess."

"Quite," murmured the Professor. To himself he added, "I wonder if the murderer sees his mistake yet?"

Whom did Fordney suspect? What mistake did he make? Turn page for solution.

• • • • **THE ENGLISH MR. BARRET** • • • •

". . . I was first mate at the time. My, how that old boat rolled and tossed. First to the right, then to the left. Able seaman that I was, it fair 'put the wind up' me. I was standing near the front and had just started for the back of the boat when a bloody wave thirty feet high hit us almost broadside and I was thrown against a life-boat. Broke a leg, I did. Smashed two ribs and got this ugly scar on my forehead," continued the garrulous passenger who had been regaling the Professor with his adventures.

Fordney was on a mission to Buenos Aires and had hoped (quite futilely it seemed) to keep his identity unknown. To his annoyance he had been recognized by this talkative shipmate, while taking a stroll.

The usually amiable and genial Professor was ordinarily fond of society, but on this voyage he would have preferred being left alone. He was tired and a bit fed up.

"And then . . ." but this time he interrupted his companion.

"English, aren't you, Mr. Barret?"

"I'm not the one to deny that," came the rather bellicose reply.

"Well, you'll pardon me, Mr. Barret," Fordney emphasized the name slightly. "Here's my cabin . . . I have some writing to do."

"Righto! See you in the lounge at tea-time." The Pro-

Solution — The Call of Death

According to the evidence Lil did not handle the cocktail shaker while Rowel was in the apartment, yet her fingerprints were on it, under Rowel's prints. From this fact, Fordney knew that Rowel must have returned to the apartment during Manfield's absence, wiped the shaker clean, pressed Lil's fingers to it, then handled it freely himself. Unable to account for his prints over the girl's Rowel confessed. He made the fake phone call to Manfield, watched him leave, returned to the apartment and killed Lil in a jealous rage. To restore his shattered nerves, he drank from the shaker, then in panic wiped it clean. Finally he recalled that his prints should be on it. Then in an effort to keep Lil "in character" he put the shaker in her dead hands (while still holding it in a towel), then handled it freely himself. Had he simply put Lil's hands about it after he had handled it, there would have been no suspicion.

IT IS TOO LATE TO BE ON OUR GUARD WHEN WE ARE IN THE MIDST OF EVIL — Seneca

fessor closed his stateroom door with a sigh, threw himself on the bed.

"A first mate!" he scoffed. "Let's see now. Barret. English. The man's a rank impostor!"

Fordney dozed.

How did the Professor know "Mr. Barret" was an impostor? Turn page for solution.

Turn page for solution.

• DETECTIVE ADAMS'S QUICK PERCEPTION •

"You know, Jim," soliloquized Fordney, "I've got some pretty smart boys in that class of mine! It's gratifying to see the strides most of them are making."

"You're like an old hen with her chicks," retorted Kelley, squinting at his friend through cigar smoke. "What mental Herculean feat has one of them accomplished now, may I ask?"

The Professor chuckled good-naturedly. "You know how I've drilled the importance of observation into them—well, the Carter arrest was the result of that. It wasn't a serious affair, but it might have been.

"Detectives Charles Adams and Bill Jeffries were driving their squad car towards the air base. It was 7:45 A.M. on a Sunday during the last World War and both boys were tired from the long hours of night duty. Suddenly Charley, turning to his companion and pointing to a passing car, asked, 'What's wrong with it?'

" 'Nothing,' sleepily retorted Jeffries. The car's occupants, an elderly man driving and a boy sitting in the middle of the back seat, his lips puckered in a whistle, were rambling along at a leisurely pace—both ordinary, unsuspicious-looking individuals! Also everything about the old open Ford was in order. Yet Adams knew something was wrong!

"Motioning the car to the curb he discovered two ten-gallon cans of airplane gas on the floor between the front and back seats!"

"Oh, Adams just had a hunch," grunted Kelley. "Why did they stop the car?"

"Because of my drilling the importance of observation into my boys!" retorted Fordney.

What observation aroused Adams's suspicion? Turn page for solution.

* * * * * * **CLASS DAY** * * * * * *

"While strolling along the avenue last Sunday I stopped in front of a familiar edifice and my thoughts flew back to the day the cornerstone was laid. I read it again:

> **AND MOSES SAID**
> **FOR TODAY IS**
> **A SABBATH UNTO THE LORD**
> **A. D. 1901**

Solution — *The English Mr. Barret*

Fordney knew that "Mr. Barret" had never been a sailor. No seaman refers to the left, right or front or back of a boat. The unvarying nautical terminology of the sea is port, starboard, forward, aft and ship.

THERE SHOULD ALWAYS BE SOME FOUNDATION OF FACT FOR THE MOST AIRY FABRIC — *Byron*

"You were there, Jim, but you wouldn't remember," smiled the Professor, turning to one of his students at the University. "You were a tot of two, clinging to Kelley's neck. In those days Kelley was just a flatfoot who was constantly chiding me about my ambitions to become a criminologist!

"Samuel Rosemann was also with us. We three had been pals since grade school. How little did any of us realize, that day, what our futures would be! Kelley, Inspector of Police; Rosemann, rabbi of that very temple, which by the way is still considered one of the finest in the country, and I—a criminologist—teaching you fellows the science of crime detection!

"It has been several years since I heard Rosemann speak. I must attend one of his services in the near future. But reminiscing won't get us on with our day's work.

"Jim, I want you to sum up briefly the important facts of Colonel Goddard's last lecture on bullet identification."

"Why . . . why . . . I haven't had a chance to study my notes, Professor. I thought you'd give us a few more days on that. However, you didn't catch me off guard with that yarn. I've learned your reminiscences generally carry a point for us and the point of that one is . . ."

What is it? Turn page for solution.

• • • • • • **DOWNUNDERS** • • • • • •

A beatific smile spread over the broad Celtic features of Inspector James Aloysius Kelley as he completed his laborious efforts. How he had sweated over it, but for once he'd take a bit of professorial wind out of his friend!

"Come in! Come in!" boomed James Aloysius at Fordney's knock. "Take a pew, take a pew, Joe. Just completing my report on that Sandow caper. Want to hear it?"

The Professor nodded—warily. The Inspector was up to something.

"Listen," said Kelley. "This slick mob of jewel thieves and blackmailers is composed of Myra Bartell, Angus Hart, Alex Tomer and Mona Jallona—all Australians. One of the men is bald-headed, one has an artificial leg. The following is additionally enlightening:

1. Alex Tomer, a diabetic, and the mob front play brilliant chess. Mona and her gang boy-friend also play a sound game but are more expert in gin rummy.

2. The gang leader, the front and Angus Hart are linguists. The leader speaks fluent Spanish and Portuguese; the front, French and Polish; and Hart, German and Bohemian.

3. Last week the gang leader and the front bought Mona a red motorcycle.

Solution — Detective Adams's Quick Perception

Charley Adams knew from experience and observation that normally a boy will not sit in the back seat of a car when its only other occupant is the driver.

EXPERIENCE IS RETROSPECT KNOWLEDGE — Ballou

Solution — Class Day

The cornerstone of a synagogue would never bear the inscription A.D. The year 1901 A.D. is, in the Jewish calendar, the year 5661.

THE JEWS! THEY DATE BEYOND THE PYRAMIDS — Lamb

4. Recently at a Notre Dame football game a dick tailing Myra Bartell overheard her tell the leader that she'd met a professional pretzel-bender whom she simply adored.

"That's all," smiled Kelley. "I rounded up the mob and they're in the cooler. Of course one with your vast erudition and instant perception will know who the leader and the front are!"

"Quite," chuckled the Professor, handing Kelley their names.

Who is the leader? Who is the front? Turn page for solution.

• • INCIDENT OF THE HUNGRY CORPSE • •

As Sergeant Cargo released the bolt on the trap door in the stone floor of the huge unused storeroom, Professor Fordney observed a curious expression on Hannah Deegle's face. The old servant's raised hand fell to her side as she turned toward the kitchen.

In a corner of the huge, dark, rat-infested cellar they found Oren Badger sitting in a decrepit rocking chair, a bullet in his head, a revolver on the floor.

Strewn about on all sides was food; raw and cooked meat, vegetables, cheese. The heel of Badger's left foot, which had been gnawed to the bone, indicated what would have happened without such provender. Badger had been dead about three days.

* * *

On a long table in the wealthy recluse's library Fordney found his will, mortgages, bonds, insurance policies and considerable cash neatly stacked. A large piece of paper bearing the scrawled words, ALL IN ORDER, lay on top of the pile.

Cargo barely succeeded in choking off a startled protest as the Professor removed a bundle of bills and slipped it into his pocket as Hannah entered. She repeated her story. Badger, in ill health for months, had several times threatened suicide. She had left Sunday at 3 o'clock and on his orders had not returned until that Wednesday morning at 7. Failing to find him, she notified the police.

"I ain't surprised he killed himself," Hannah concluded.

"Mr. Badger was murdered," quietly said Fordney.

What clue spelled murder to the Professor? Turn page for solution.

• • • • **CALLING SQUAD CAR 18** • • • •

The stick-ups during the last month had got Inspector Kelley's goat; he asked Fordney to ride a squad car with him. As the Professor was aroused by the recent crime wave, he assented.

With Sergeant Reynolds driving, the three set out from headquarters at 11 P.M., with rain swirling from every di-

---

Solution — Downunders

1. The front is not Alex Tomer.
2. Angus Hart is neither the leader nor the front.
3. Mona Jallona is neither leader nor front.
4. Myra Bartell is not the leader. Therefore Alex Tomer is the leader and Myra Bartell the front.

MANY ARE DESTINED TO REASON WRONGLY — *Voltaire*

rection, blown by the shifting wind. Lightning flashed and thunder boomed.

The first call to their car, repeated three times, was: "Car 18 investigate robbery, first floor apartment, 2088 Leopold Boulevard. WPPJ."

Reynolds stepped on it, and with siren shrieking the car speeded through the stormy night.

Arriving at the scene they found two excited young women, one blonde, the other brunette. While Fordney questioned the blonde, Kelley interrogated the brunette. The blonde stated she was a collector for an ice cream company. She said that she had visited a number of stores collecting for deliveries during the day. They both said that as their car drew up in front of the apartment two men jumped on either running board of the sedan and jammed guns in their ribs, demanding the money. The brunette handed it over.

Fordney learned that the last collection, and their last stop, was made about a mile away.

He noticed the two large diamonds on the blonde's hand and said: "I'm afraid, girls, we'll have to take you to headquarters."

Why did Fordney think the alleged robbery was faked? Turn page for solution.

· · · · · **A TRAGIC QUARREL** · · · · ·

"It was horrible, being so close and still unable to save her!" Ben Jordan falteringly told Professor Fordney. "I was walking up the garden path toward the house when I saw her, through the window, stand on the stool, throw the rope over the beam, knot it, and then jump off. When I reached her I was so horrified I fainted. When I regained consciousness I was afraid of being accused of murdering her, but when I came to my senses I cut her down and notified the police."

While the beam from which Jordan said his wife hanged herself was unmarked, Fordney quickly noticed the heel prints on the overturned three-legged stool. The knot, still in the one inch rope, had marked the woman's beautiful throat. He also knew the rope had been freshly cut—no mistake about that.

"If only I hadn't gone for a walk after our quarrel," continued Jordan, "this tragedy would never have happened!"

The Professor examined the corpse. Symptoms of hanging were visible, face bluish in color, froth on the mouth, and tongue protruding.

Solution — Incident of the Hungry Corpse

Fordney found the cellar trap door bolted.

BUT FACTS ARE CHIELS THAT DINNA DING, AND DONNA BE DISPUTED — Robert Burns

Solution — Calling Squad Car 18

The Professor later proved the robbery a fake because both girls said the stick-up men jammed guns against their ribs. He knew that in the swirling rain they would not have been driving with their windows down. Had they not been down the alleged robbers could not have stuck the guns against their bodies.

GUILT SOON LEARNS TO LIE — Braddon

"As a routine question, Jordan," he asked, "did you meet anyone on your walk who could prove your alibi?"

"Why . . . no . . . not that I am conscious of . . . I was upset . . ."

"You murdered your wife!" Fordney stated emphatically, staring at the man's shoes.

How did he know? Turn page for solution.

• • • DEATH IN THE MOUNTAINS • • •

While hunting in the Adirondacks, Fordney was informed of a tragedy at one of the camps. Thinking he might be of some help, he went over and introduced himself and was told of the accident by Wylie, the victim's companion.

"When Moore hadn't returned to camp at nine o'clock last night, I was a bit worried, because he didn't know these mountains. There wasn't a star out and it was dark and moonless, so I decided to look around for him. We're five miles from anyone, you know.

"Putting more wood on the fire, I set out. After searching for an hour I was coming up the slope of a ravine when I saw a pair of eyes shining at me.

"Calling twice, and getting no answer, I fired, thinking it was a mountain lion. Imagine my horror when I reached the spot, struck a match, and saw I had nearly blown off Moore's head. A terrible experience!

"I carried him back to camp and then walked to the nearest house to report the accident."

"How far from camp did you find him?"

"About a quarter of a mile."

"How did you manage to shoot with your right hand bandaged?"

"Oh—I use either hand."

"Mind if I look at the gun?"

"Not at all." Wylie handed it over.

"H'mmmm. European make. Had it long?"

"No. It's rather new."

"Why did you deliberately murder Moore?" Fordney abruptly demanded. "For that's what you did!"

How did he know? Turn page for solution.

• • • •   THE COLOR OF MURDER   • • • •

The room was a shambles. Arlene Brewster had fought valiantly, but now her beaten, battered body lay dead on the bed. It was vicious, insensate murder. The open window onto the fire escape spoke mutely.

The Professor removed his hat, dripping from the steady rain. He got to his knees, crawled from one irregularly-shaped, bluish-colored spot on the floor to another. They were about the size of a dime. H'mmm. The criminologist toyed with his ear lobe. He was puzzled. Then he "got the picture."

Solution — A Tragic Quarrel

The Professor was confident that Jordan had murdered his wife because there was no rope mark on the beam from which he said he saw her hang herself. Had she done so there would have been. Fordney later proved Jordan had strangled her with the rope and faked the scene.

Four hardened suspects were brought in for grilling: Joe Maxon, Roy Young, Gig Putnam and Dave Rubin. One of the four had been out of prison only ten days after doing nine years.

Before the interrogation began Fordney picked up the following meager facts:

1. The underworld was unusually cooperative because the murderer, who had been in the city only a short time, was not one of them.

2. In a search of Dave Rubin's apartment in the swank Dresden Arms where he had lived luxuriously ever since the unsolved Washburton jewel robbery three years before, Fordney found a startling clue to that puzzling crime.

3. Gig Putnam denied that he had fingered Roy Young, a hoodlum with eight local arrests, when Young's cousin, Paul Bruce, accused him of doing so. Bruce said Putnam was motivated by Young's persistent refusal to let his sister join a local gang of female blackmailers which Putnam had headed for two years.

From the above Fordney knew the name of the murderer, that he wore poorly dyed, blue socks and had a hole in his shoe.

Who was the murderer? Turn page for solution.

Who was the murderer? Turn page for solution.

• • • • • •   CASE #99   • • • • • • •

Doctor Chester's report in part confirmed Henry Hobb's story. It stated that, while Irma Hobb's body bore several cuts and bruises, the cause of death was a downward blow on her temple, where she had apparently hit herself on the corner of a mahogany chest. Death had probably resulted an hour afterwards. He could not definitely say there was no poison in the body until after the autopsy.

Hobb and his wife lived in a small house in an isolated part of the country and, so far as anyone knew, enjoyed that greatest of blessings, marital felicity.

One afternoon in late November Hobb rushed to the police station of the small adjacent town and said his wife was dead. He told the officer that on returning home he found Mrs. Hobb, scratched and bruised, lying in a daze

---

Solution — *Death in the Mountains*

It was a dark, starless, moonless night. No animal's eyes shine in the dark unless there is a light that can be reflected from them. A human's eyes NEVER shine under any circumstances.

Wylie could not possibly have seen eyes shining at him in the dark. It was clearly murder.

AND THY DEEP EYES, AMID THE GLOOM, SHINE LIKE JEWELS IN A SHROUD — *Longfellow*

Solution — *The Color of Murder*

As the murderer had been in the city only a short time, we know (3) that Gig Putnam is not the killer, as he had lived there for at least two years.

As Dave Rubin (2) had lived at the Dresden Arms for three years, he is eliminated as the murderer.

Roy Young also had lived in the city for some time (3), so he, too, was eliminated, leaving Joe Maxon as the brutal murderer.

on the davenport. He had rushed upstairs to the bathroom for some aromatic spirits of ammonia, hoping thus to arouse her. On returning to the first floor he found her reeling around and before he could catch her she fell forward, striking her temple on the low chest which stood in the hallway. Having no telephone, he tried to revive her with such medicines as were at hand. Failing to do so and finally realizing she was dead, he had gone for the police.

After examining Mrs. Hobb's nails, Professor Fordney remarked: "Doctor Chester, you will have to revise your report. Hobb will be held!"

Why? Turn page for solution.

Why? Turn page for solution.

• • • • THE SECRETARY'S STORY • • • •

The Professor carefully picked up a letter lying near a revolver beside the dead man, and held it to the light. The watermark on the sheet of fine, smooth, uncreased paper of excellent quality, $7\frac{1}{2}$ by 11 inches, was plainly visible, proving that the paper, while similar in appearance and texture to that found in Leopold's desk, was not the same.

Fordney murmured something to himself and rang for the dead man's secretary.

"Now, Willard, let's have your story."

"Well, first of all, Professor, I have absolutely no idea why Mr. Leopold committed suicide. He has been in unusually good spirits of late and was keenly anticipating a trip abroad next week."

The secretary went on to say that after opening the afternoon mail which brought the letter Fordney had so carefully examined, he had taken it to his employer in the study. About an hour later, desiring some information, he returned to the room and found Leopold sitting in front of an open window staring at the garden, a dark, brooding scowl on his face. Receiving no reply to his question Willard looked closer and discovered him dead! Yes, the two men were alone in the house at the time.

Fordney again studied the letter with its large, bold feminine handwriting which definitely ended a love affair with Leopold. It was signed L. B.

"Who is L. B.?" he suddenly demanded.

"Why . . . Miss Benedict," Willard replied with slight hesitation.

"Come, tell me the truth about this affair!" Fordney demanded.

How did Fordney know the secretary was lying? Turn page for solution.

Solution — Case #99

If Mrs. Hobb had hit her temple on the low chest in falling forward, the direction of the blow would have been upward. Hobb's story was thus disproved.

O VILLAINY! HO! LET THE DOOR BE LOCK'D; TREACHERY! SEEK IT OUT — Shakespeare

---

Professor Fordney saw his quarry coming toward him and he admired the artistry of the man's disguise. Limping along, cane in right hand, to a less astute person he would have passed for Doctor Bellen. The impeccable attire, the white goatee, even the mannerisms of the great and eccentric surgeon were perfectly simulated. Yet Fordney penetrated the disguise and recognized the man as William Barstow, one of the greatest living actors. Although in his prime, his star had set and he had recently given way to younger but much less capable actors. The criminologist allowed himself a moment of philosophical reflection on fleeting fame before trailing his man.

The Professor's curiosity was aroused. He was determined to learn the connection between the false Doctor Bellen, and the true one who had been so mysteriously shot and seriously wounded in the left leg several days before. Even the police didn't know of the incident as yet. For some reason the surgeon obviously wanted to hide the fact that his wound was serious. Inquiries at his house always brought the information that the doctor was out. That, reasoned the Professor, was why he had employed Barstow to appear in public and at those places habitually frequented by him.

As "Doctor Bellen" was about to enter his club Fordney touched him on the shoulder. The man turned with that sharp piercing glance well known to the surgeon's associates and patients.

"Well . . ." he demanded.

Fordney smiled. "Even geniuses make mistakes," he remarked cryptically. "Except for one you made I wouldn't have known you are not Doctor Bellen."

What mistake had Barstow made? Turn page for solution.

"Gee, Professor, that was a tough session," sighed George Adams, perching himself on the edge of the desk and inhaling deeply from the cigaret just lighted.

"I'll say it was," added Sergeant Reynolds. The class was enjoying a fifteen-minute recess from its monthly examination.

"You're getting lazy," chided Fordney. "Here's a simple little problem for you two fellows that should step you up mentally.

Solution — The Secretary's Story

Fordney found the letter, which the secretary said he had opened and taken to his employer, uncreased. As the sheet was 7½ by 11 inches Fordney knew that had it arrived by post it would have been folded.

THE LETTER IS TOO LONG BY HALF A MILE — *Shakespeare*

Solution — Professor Fordney's Curiosity

The real Doctor Bellen had been seriously wounded in the left leg a few days before. Therefore, if he had been in physical condition to get about, he would (even despite habit) have carried his cane in his left hand to take the weight off the injured leg. Barstow's one mistake was in carrying the cane in his right hand.

HE WHO WOULD PRY BEHIND THE SCENES OFT SEES A COUNTERFEIT — *Dryden*

"Yesterday morning a customer walked into Sam Smith's and bought a $5 hat, giving in payment a $20 bill. Sam had only another $20 bill in his cash register, so he hurried next door to Johnson's book store with the customer's $20 bill and asked Johnson to kindly change it. Johnson gave Sam four $5 bills, saying he was going to the bank in a few minutes and would get some change for himself.

"Sam returned to his own store, gave the man $15 change and the customer walked out with the hat on his head.

"Thirty minutes later Johnson rushed into Sam's store, excitedly exclaiming, 'That $20 bill you gave me was counterfeit! The bank clerk caught it and refused to give me change or to return the $20 bill.'

"Sam was amazed and chagrined, but assured Johnson he would not lose by the deal. 'I gave my customer his $15 and he's gone, so there's nothing for me to do but give you the $20 bill I have in my register. Kind of tough break for me right now, but . . .' "

How much did Sam lose? Quickly now! Turn page for solution.

• • • • • •   KILL CRAZY   • • • • • • •

Professor Fordney, applying the new science of endocrine-criminology, studied photos of the four brutish faces. All of them were killers, but one ruthlessly and without reason had shot to death his friend, Sheriff Dan Flynn.

For ten days the kill-crazy mob had wantonly maimed and murdered, had terrorized the northwestern part of the state. The four vicious killers were Moxie Mogg, Pinky Hunt, Mike Cleary and Jake Barron.

Applying his knowledge of endocrine-criminology to the photos, Fordney picked the likely leader. Confident that he would attempt a sensational break-through he ordered a close road block, then he and his men closed in, narrowing the gang's area of operation.

Caught in a police trap, the four killed two more men before they were captured. Sullen and defiant they refused to talk. From certain sources, however, Fordney learned the following:

1. One of the four always carries a knife instead of a gun.
2. Hunt's uncle is a fence and married to the sister of the man who killed Sheriff Flynn. The knife-carrier and Hunt are blond.
3. Moxie Mogg and the knife-carrier had great confidence in Barron's driving ability and insisted against the killer's mild objection that he devote himself exclusively to driving the mob's getaway car.
4. The knife-carrier and Flynn's assassin have been friends for years.
5. Recently Barron and the killer pulled a stick-up unknown to the other two.

Armed with his data Professor Fordney had the murderer of Sheriff Flynn dragged from his cell and brought before him.

Who killed Sheriff Flynn? Turn page for solution.

Solution — Class Day

Sam lost $15 and the hat.

100

Chief Detective Inspector Horace Huntly of Scotland Yard, visiting the United States on a confidential mission, closely examined the bullet hole in the lower pane of the study window. He stepped back and gauged the angle of fire. "Quite so," he murmured.

Professor Fordney and the chief inspector found the lights off in the Connecticut study of Leslie Melton, the mysterious South African. The shades were lowered halfway over closed windows. Melton's corpse was slumped in a chair by an east window. A .45 caliber bullet had gone through Melton's head and the window glass behind him. The shot was fired from the left of the body between 9:30 and 10:30 P.M. It was now 11:55.

Fordney handed the .45 caliber revolver he picked up from the floor to the chief inspector, parted the curtains, raised the shade and stabbed a beam from his flashlight at a second recently-made bullet hole near the top of the upper windowpane.

"Extraordinary," said Chief Inspector Huntly. "Only one shot has been fired from this gun, so . . ."

"And here it is," announced Sergeant Cargo, entering the room. "Found it in the flower bed outside the window. It's a .45—from that gun all right."

"But," interjected the chief inspector, "two shots must have been fired even though appearances of the gun indicate otherwise. Better look about for that second bullet, sergeant."

"That won't be necessary," said the Professor.

"But I don't understand," Huntly exclaimed.

"It's quite obvious," Fordney chuckled. "Only one shot was fired."

What is your explanation of the single shot and the

two bullet holes in the windowpane? Turn page for solution.

Turn page for solution.

• • • AN INTERVIEW WITH DEATH • • •

"Yes, one does run into unique conspiracies in my work," the Professor remarked over after-dinner coffee. "Here is what gave me the lead in that Carobus case you all found so interesting," he continued, handing one of his guests the following classified newspaper advertisement.

WANTED: Confidential private secretary. Unusual salary and opportunity for young man speaking Russian. Culture and refinement necessary qualifications. Address Box KR. 165.

Solution — Kill Crazy

1. The knife-carrier is not the killer as Sheriff Flynn was shot.

2. Hunt is not the knife-carrier or the killer.

3. Moxie Mogg is not the knife-carrier. Jake Barron is not the knife-carrier or the murderer.

4. The knife-carrier and killer are friends. Hence, as Barron and Hunt are neither knife-carrier or murderer, and as Mogg is not the knife-carrier, Moxie Mogg is the murderer.

Therefore, Mike Cleary is the knife-carrier.

MURDER MAY PASS UNPUNISHED FOR A TIME, BUT TARDY JUSTICE WILL O'ERTAKE THE CRIME — Dryden

"I don't see how that gave you any information. Looks all right to me," his guest reported, passing on the clipping.

"Well," Fordney continued, "that ad furnished the strongest link in my chain of evidence. I had previous information that Jack Hemwell was infatuated with Carobus's wife. At the suggestion of Mrs. Carobus her husband answered this ad, and received a reply requesting him to call for a personal interview. That interview was with death!

"Mrs. Carobus, when questioned, said that she and her husband had not been on particularly friendly terms recently and that the last she saw of him was when he left for Swampscott to see about the position.

"I had called at the newspaper office and was informed that the ad had been inserted by Gerald Kesl, Hotel DuBarry. They remembered the ad because, while Mr. Kesl had phoned to ascertain if there were any replies and was informed there were, they had not been called for. At the Hotel DuBarry I found Kesl was unknown.

"I learned from Mrs. Carobus that her husband had answered the ad in longhand and that he was left-handed and a very poor penman.

"Pondering the matter, though puzzled at first, I finally hit upon the manner in which Carobus had been led to his death."

"I don't see how!" Doris Jopke said with a perplexed frown.

Do you? Turn page for solution.

* * *

"Well, Inspector, we finally caught Newman," said Fordney as he walked into Kelley's office. "He gave us quite a chase, though! What a cold, heartless murderer

Solution — A Visit from Scotland Yard

The single shot went through the window glass while the lower pane was raised or the upper pane lowered—or both were moved. After the shot was fired the window was closed, thus accounting for the bullet hole in upper and lower panes.

THE TRUTH IS TOO SIMPLE FOR US — Alkilexi

Solution — An Interview with Death

No one called at the newspaper office for the answers to the advertisement, yet Carobus received a reply to his letter of application. As Gerald Kesl, the placer of the ad, was unknown, the name was fictitious. The ad was answered by Carobus at his wife's suggestion. Therefore, the only possible solution is that she acquainted her lover, Hemwell, with the fact that her husband had answered the ad, and he (Hemwell), without calling for the replies to his ad at the newspaper office, wrote Carobus arranging the meeting at which he was killed.

THE GREAT ART IN WRITING ADVERTISEMENT IS THE FINDING OUT A PROPER METHOD TO CATCH THE READER'S EYE — Addison

he is! He calmly ate his dinner while planning the crime.

"He didn't give the restaurant manager a chance," Fordney continued, "just brutally shot him in cold blood —and all for $60. I tell you, Jim, murderers don't need much incentive! After killing him he made a fast getaway in a waiting car.

"Fortunately a detective was having dinner in the restaurant at the time and gave orders that nothing was to be disturbed at the table where Newman had eaten. Caught by surprise he was unable to apprehend the killer.

"I've examined that table carefully and while we have several witnesses who will swear to the man's identity, including the waitress who served him, no jury will convict on that alone.

"While I found none of the suspect's fingerprints, personal effects or physical traces at, or on, the table, that little table is going to prove our man is a ruthless murderer and that he calmly premeditated this outrage while eating his dinner."

"I hope you're right, Joe," responded Kelley, "but both Newman and his attorney seem very confident we have nothing on him."

"No? Well, the prosecution will have little difficulty in proving that Newman premeditated the crime, and he'll undoubtedly be sentenced on a first degree murder charge!"

How did the Professor know Newman had deliberately planned the crime? Turn page for solution.

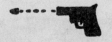

The Professor sighed. At last he had located one of Herman Hohlman's addresses. Now it was but a question of time before the suspected Nazi agent would be in custody. But was the well-to-do Gunther family, with whom he roomed, aware of Hohlman's real identity as Carl Brugg? Were they actively assisting him? Or were they completely innocent? He wouldn't question the Gunthers when he searched Hohlman's room. Perhaps close observation would disclose the answer.

* * *

"I am amazed at what you tell me, Professor," attractive Mrs. Evelyn Gunther said as the two mounted the stairs. "Mr. Hohlman said he was a traveling accountant. And he seemed such a nice, gentlemanly sort of person we took him in because of the housing shortage. This is his room, though he's been away for three days and no one has been in it since he left."

Solution — First Degree Murder

No fingerprints were found on anything at the table! Fordney knew immediately that the murderer, Newman, had contemplated the crime, or he would have had no object in obliterating his fingerprints. Identification being proved, the Professor believed a first degree verdict would be rendered. It was.

WHATEVER THOUGHTS THE NERVES OF MOTIVE, WHATEVER SHIFTS MAN'S MORAL POSITION, IS MIGHTIER THAN STEAM OR CALORIC OR LIGHTNING — *Chapin*

The Professor had hardly begun his search of Hohlman's room when he was startled by the ringing of a bell attached to the single bed. Its loud peals continued until he discovered it was connected to an alarm clock on the bedside table. He pushed in the alarm button and continued his search. Among other things he found, under the carpet, a faded photograph of a striking girl of about twenty. Was she Mrs. Gunther? Another item aroused his speculation —a tiny hourglass. This he discovered in a secret writing-table drawer. Thoughtfully he went downstairs. Mrs. Gunther had lied to him, therefore she must be involved in Hohlman's activities.

Why did the Professor suspect Mrs. Gunther? How did he know she had lied? Turn page for solution.

• • • • • **THE FORGERY RING** • • • • •

If one of the mob had not turned to quick, savage murder, it is doubtful that the Professor would have been concerned in the affairs of the most successful forgery ring in years. But when Winston C. Brandon was brutally beaten to death, after apparently recognizing at least one of the forgery ring, the criminologist was asked to assist in finding his murderer. The members of the ring were: Eric Doggin, Arnold Maine, David Ridley, and Monty Crandall.

Because the exceedingly astute forgers had little underworld association and were most circumspect in their conduct Fordney found it extremely difficult to obtain information concerning any of them. However, he did manage to pick up the following unrelated facts:

1. Eric Doggin's cousin and the killer's niece (their only female relatives) had attended the same finishing school. The ring's passer of forged checks and documents was madly infatuated with Doggin's cousin.

2. Arnold Maine and the passer had good reason to believe that David Ridley was the cleverest penman in the country. His forgeries had passed many experts without detection.

3. A few days before Winston Brandon was killed David Ridley was secretly married to a respectable girl who knew nothing of his criminal occupation. The day after the wedding she accidentally learned of his activities and begged him to discontinue his crime career. The day of the murder Ridley told the killer and the passer he was through.

Armed with the above, police spread a dragnet for the gang with instructions from Fordney to be especially alert in picking up the killer and the ring's passer.

Who is the killer? Who is the passer? Turn page for solution.

Solution — Incident of the Amazed Housekeeper

Mrs. Gunther said Hohlman had been away three days and that no one had been in his room, yet the bell controlled by the alarm clock rang! This meant that someone (Hohlman as was later proved) had been in the room during the past thirty-six hours and wound the alarm clock. Otherwise it would have run down and could not have rung the bell.

THE CLOCK UPBRAIDS ME — Shakespeare

"Only the 6th of July and you're back in New York!" Fordney remarked as Pelnar stepped from the plane at the airport. "Thought you intended spending the summer in Cuba?"

"Well, if you must know why I'm here, my bank failed and I came back to straighten out my affairs."

"That's tough. How did you hear about it?"

Pelnar handed Fordney a clipping from the Jacksonville Herald:

> New York, July 5 (AP)—City Bank & Trust Company, one of New York's oldest banking establishments, closed its doors today. . . .

"Sure you didn't come back to help your pal, Moore?" the criminologist asked. "He's been in jail for two days . . . ever since the Fourth of July bombing. Had a letter on him signed by you asking him to get in touch with L. J. Maguire.

"We traced Maguire and discovered he is with an ammunition company. When the District Attorney heard you were on your way here he asked me to meet the plane. He's confident you know something about the bombing . . . and so am I!"

"Didn't know there was a bombing! What's it all about? Maguire is a cousin of mine—and you say Moore's in the can?"

"Right! Where did you catch your plane?"

"Why . . . er . . . Jacksonville. You see, I was staying at a remote place . . . no planes serve that part of the island. I had no thought of leaving until I read of the bank failure. Then I hopped a boat, grabbed a plane, and here I am."

"No—that won't do," Fordney retorted. "Your alibi is darn weak."

"Weak! What do you mean! I suppose somebody wired the D.A. that 'Crazy' Kirby met the plane when we landed in Norfolk for gas. In spite of that there's nothing on me!"

Why did the Professor know that Pelnar's story was wrong? Turn page for solution.

• • • • **DEATH OF THE ACTOR** • • • •

Entering the dressing room of Hilary Mantell, lionized matinee idol, Professor Fordney observed the cracked mirror of the dressing table directly opposite the door, glanced at the dead body of Gerald Hooper, then became interested in the gun lying on the carpet and a shattered jar of cold cream lying in the corner.

Solution — The Forgery Ring

1. Eric Doggin is neither killer nor passer. We also learn that the killer is not the passer.
2. Arnold Maine is neither the passer nor the penman.
3. David Ridley is neither passer nor killer.

Eric Doggin is not the killer or the passer. David Ridley is neither passer, nor killer. Therefore, as Arnold Maine is not the passer, he is the killer and, as the others have been eliminated, Monty Crandall is the passer.

HIS UNDERSTANDING AT BEST IS OF THE MIDDLING SIZE — Swift

The two burly policemen stood guard at the door that swung to behind the Professor, Inspector Kelley and Doctor Lyman.

While the physician made his examination Kelley questioned Mantell, whom they found nervously pacing the room.

"Serves him right," the actor said. "Why that fool tried to kill me, because I'm starred in this play, is beyond me. I admit he was a better actor, and I have told him so, but if the public wants me, can I help it?"

"Of course not," Kelley suavely replied. "Go on."

"Well, the door was closed and I was sitting in front of the mirror carefully applying the make-up called for in the play when suddenly a bullet whizzed past my ear. I jumped up and saw Hooper behind me. I grabbed him before he fired another shot, during which time his automatic fell to the floor. I managed to get it. He rose and hurled that cold cream jar at me, so I let him have it. It was his life or mine. There was nothing else to do, was there?"

Fordney, who had been quietly listening, said, "If your story were true you might have been justified, but in all probability it is not!"

Why did the Professor not believe Mantell? Turn page for solution.

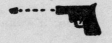

After the police photographer took a final picture of the strangled girl as she lay in the thick underbrush, Fordney removed the large, white-rimmed sunglasses from the girl's face, and the large, gaily colored kerchief which covered her head. She was an extremely beautiful brunette. From a close examination the Professor believed she had been taken by surprise and strangled from behind. As the

---

Solution — Pelnar, Moore & Maguire

Pelnar was back in New York on July 6th, two days after the Fourth of July bombing. The notice of the bank failure, appearing in the Jacksonville Herald was dated July 5th. This could not have reached Pelnar at a remote part of Cuba, unserviced by planes, in time for him to get back in New York on the 6th. His alibi, therefore, was completely broken as he said the newspaper clipping brought him back!

TIME IS THE HERALD OF TRUTH — *Cicero*

Solution — Death of the Actor

Fordney did not believe Mantell because he said that his dressing room door was closed, that he was sitting in front of the mirror carefully making up—yet he did not see Hooper enter his room, the door of which was directly behind him and the mirror. Very improbable, as Fordney said. Mantell was later convicted on charge of manslaughter. Motive? Professional jealousy.

A LIE THAT IS HALF A TRUTH IS EVER THE BLACKEST OF LIES — *Tennyson*

only contents of her shallow pockets were a package of cigarettes, a match folder, a fish hook and a dollar bill, she was not identified as dancing teacher Shirley Vie until after she had been taken to the morgue.

* * *

"Say look!" excitedly exclaimed Harry Talmadge indicating the evening newspaper. "That's the girl I saw arguing with a fellow on shore when I was fishing this afternoon."

Talmadge's companion, Joe Morrisey, looked at the photograph of the smiling Shirley in a brief dance costume.

"Come on," said Harry, "I'd better tell the cops."

* * *

". . . and that's the description of the man I saw arguing with this girl in the paper this afternoon. From what you say she must have been murdered almost immediately afterwards," Harry Talmadge concluded.

"She was," said Fordney. "Did you hear their conversation?"

"No, but his voice was loud and his manner threatening."

"Ever see Miss Vie before this afternoon?"

"No, sir."

"How far off shore were you?"

"I was in a small bay, about 200 yards away when they passed me."

"When did you cut your finger?"

"About an hour ago—when I shaved."

"That's enough," Fordney snapped. "You will be held for investigation."

Why did Fordney hold Talmadge? Turn page for solution.

"Almost everyone loves a parade," said Fordney to his students at the University ". . . and I am no exception!

"There is nothing quite so colorful as the pomp and ceremony attending the review of his Britannic Majesty's troops on the Royal birthday. A few years ago, before the war, I was fortunate enough to witness this magnificent spectacle while visiting Shepart of Scotland Yard.

"We had a box next to the Royal Family. I thrilled as the troops approached. My old friend Colonel Lawton, at the head of the Coldstream Guards, looked every inch the British soldier as he passed, controlling with a strong right arm his nervous, prancing, coal-black steed. As they came abreast, King George smiled his approval and at the same moment the Queen, turning slightly, nodded to me in recognition. Shepart whispered, 'You should feel mighty flattered, old man! Two years ago, wasn't it, when you met Her Majesty?'

Solution — Incident of the Imaginative Murder

Talmadge said he had never seen Shirley until shortly before she was murdered, at which time she wore a kerchief covering her head, and large sunglasses. Yet Talmadge "recognized" the newspaper photograph of the girl taken in brief dance costume! Knowing this would be impossible, Fordney detained him for investigation. After a sensational trial Talmadge went to the chair. He volunteered his information only because he thought he had been seen in the vicinity shortly after he killed Shirley.

THEY WHOSE GUILT WITHIN THEIR BOSOMS LIE IMAGINE EVERY EYE BEHOLDS THEIR BLAME — Shakespeare

"I nodded agreement and assured him that had I not been in his company she probably would never have remembered me. At the time I had the honor of being presented, Shepart had just completed a most delicate undertaking for Her Highness. As we were leaving the box, after the review, an attendant hastened to my side and said, 'Professor Fordney, Her Majesty would like . . .'"

"No doubt, sir," interrupted Jim Barry with an affectionate grin, "you did make quite an impression on the Queen! But you're testing our observational powers again, sir!"

The criminologist laughed. "You're improving, my boy. Go ahead, tell the class the simple flaw of common knowledge I injected into my story."

Quickly now — what was it? Turn page for solution.

Turn page for solution.

• • • • **MYSTERY IN THE ORIENT** • • • •

As the Professor sauntered through a narrow back street of Singapore, his observing eyes spotted the man, in clever disguise, whom he had trailed halfway round the world. At that moment a native plain-clothes man stepped to his side and whispered.

Fordney indicated the suspect, got into a police car and drove forty-five miles in the country. There in a roadside ditch lay the bodies of three men, their high-powered American car wrecked nearby. Two of the men were dead, the third, unconscious, was taken to a hospital.

From examination of their clothing Fordney ascertained all were U.S. citizens. Though there was no personal identification on any of them, the criminologist learned from papers in the car the three were Leonard Ball, Cedric Agar and Alfred Huntley. Among the papers was a charred check made out to Cedric Agar from the car's owner. The following is the only other information Fordney could secure from their clothing and car:

1. Leonard Ball's wife was a well-known novelist writing under a pseudonym.
2. The wife of the living man was an extremely wealthy woman who had threatened to divorce her husband if his infidelities continued.
3. The car owner had secretly encouraged her, and the living man only recently had discovered the fact.
4. Married to the survivor's wife's cousin, Leonard Ball had tried to effect a reconciliation between the survivor and his wife, and had upbraided the car owner, engaged to a planter's daughter, for his attitude.

Fordney checked his notes, then sent a cable to the living man's wife.

Who is the survivor of the accident? Turn page for solution.

Solution — Class Day

No cavalry man ever holds the reins in his right hand. If he did, how could he salute or use his weapons?

FAMILIARITY SO DULLS THE EDGE OF PERCEPTION AS TO MAKE US LEAST ACQUAINTED WITH THINGS FORMING PART OF OUR DAILY LIVES — Howe

---

"I killed old Tad Buller last Wednesday night—shot him in self-defense," desert rat Alex Morse calmly told Sheriff Dawson. "Buried him next mornin', then took sick so couldn't come in before." Sheriff Dawson and Professor Fordney reached for their hats. This was Tuesday.

* * *

From the shallow desert grave they lifted the mattress on which lay Tad Buller's body, a pillow between his legs, a hole in his chest and head. He was dressed in long, dirty underwear.

"That's him all right," volunteered Buller's nephew. "He always slept in his underwear and he couldn't sleep without a pillow between his legs to ease the pain of his hernia." Doctor Walsh nodded in confirmation. Fordney's eyes swept the desert floor.

The party visited Buller's shack, returned to the Sheriff's office. Alex was retelling his story.

"Old Tad's been gettin' cantankerous as hell. We was ready for bed. Suddenly Tad runs to the porch and dashes back into the house with his revolver, cursin' and accusin' me of knowin' where he's buried his money. Said he was goin' to kill me. I reached my rifle as he fired and missed. He fired again. Then I had to let him have it—twice. He fell on the bed dead. I buried him in the mornin'. The rest you know."

Fordney recalled the blood stains in the shack; the broken window. Also that there was a leak in the roof over Tad's bed. He nodded approval as Sheriff Dawson said: "You didn't shoot in self-defense, Morse, you murdered your partner!"

How did Fordney and Dawson know Morse did not kill Buller in self-defense? Turn page for solution.

Professor Fordney and Inspector Kelley hurried into the apartment, stopped abruptly in the living room and took in the scene.

Fordney picked up a handbag lying on the floor to the right of Beverly Loman's pajama-clad body, unclasped it and was about to speak when Kelley observed:

Solution — Mystery in the Orient

The charred note made out to Cedric Agar by the car's owner establishes the owner as either Leonard Ball or Alfred Huntley.

As we find in (4) that Leonard Ball is not the car owner, we know that Alfred Huntley is.

In (1) and (2) we see that the still living man and Ball are married while (3) and (4) show that the car owner is unmarried.

Consequently Alfred Huntley (the unmarried man) is not the survivor and as Leonard Ball is eliminated as the living man in (4) the survivor is Cedric Agar.

A GOOD HEAD CANNOT READ AMISS — *Emerson*

Solution — Incident of the Sick Murderer

They knew Morse lied, that he did not shoot Buller during a gun battle but when Buller was sleeping, for the pillow which he habitually used in sleeping was between his legs! Morse was hanged.

SHAKE OFF THIS DOWNY SLEEP, DEATH'S COUNTERFEIT, AND LOOK UPON DEATH ITSELF — *Shakespeare*

"From the position of her body it looks as though she was kneeling on that footstool when shot. Kneeling!"

As the Inspector examined the body the Professor withdrew a freely bloodstained, engraved card from the handbag. It read: ROGER HILL. Below this in pencil was: *CUT OUT THIS PIXIE BUSINESS OR . . .*

Kelley held up a revolver. "Shot through the heart; blasted it to pieces. While it could be suicide, I . . . say, what's that you've got?"

Fordney handed him the card.

* * *

"Today is Beverly's birthday. I stopped at Saks, bought her that handbag, put my card in it and ordered it delivered." Roger Hill's voice was raspy, nervous. "The message on the card? Well, a week ago Beverly and I had a spat and in a moment of pique—nothing more—she became engaged to that rat, John Butler. But I knew she didn't mean it. My note was just a bit of whimsy."

"Whimsy!" Kelley popped a jujube into his mouth, snorted. "You admit passing her apartment about the time she was killed but say you didn't go in! Why not?"

"Because I saw Butler going in. If Beverly was murdered, he did it! He knew she would break the engagement when she came to her senses!"

Kelley glanced at Fordney; the Professor stared at the ceiling.

Was it murder or suicide? If murdered, was Hill innocent? Turn page for solution.

* * *

Two shots rang through the drawing room. Eight guests laid down their bridge hands, rushed to the library.

Mrs. Sybil Morton shrieked and fainted at the sight of her daughter, Alyne, stretched on the floor. Blood from a temple wound stained her white gown. Kneeling beside the girl, Doctor Karl Orman glanced at the fatal wound and pressed the dead girl close. Sobs shook his massive body.

Lying across a windowsill, head and arms dangling outside, was the body of a roughly dressed man.

"As we entered the library," Doctor Orman told the Professor, "Alyne screamed. I was a step or two in back of her. Before I realized what was happening, the burglar knocked me down, shot Alyne and tried to escape by the window. Still a bit dazed, I rolled over on my side, pulled my gun and fired."

"And hit the mark," Fordney observed. The bullet

Solution —— It's in the Bag

Fordney believed Hill innocent because however rattled, no man would deliberately put his own bloodstained card in a handbag he had sent as a gift and leave it for the police to discover. And, as Beverly could not possibly have put it in the bag after being shot and close it (Fordney unclasped it), this was proof not only that the girl was murdered but that the killer put Hill's bloodstained card in the bag in order to frame Hill if suicide were questioned. He might have got away with it had he not closed the bag. John Butler was tried and convicted.

THERE IS NOTHING INSIGNIFICANT, NOTHING! —— Coleridge

entered the burglar's back a few inches above the heart and lodged in that organ. Death was practically instantaneous. "You were in the army, Doctor?"

"Yes. Alyne and I became engaged in London. She was a WAC."

"But," said Fordney, "I understand her reason for going to the library was to return her engagement ring to you. She kept it in the library safe. What about that?"

"A passing impulse. We'd had words. She's done it twice before. Ask her friends. They know."

"Always carry a gun?"

"Frequently. I have a permit. My slum work takes me into some pretty unsavory spots."

"Well, you'll be prescribing for the inmates of Sing Sing shortly. Unofficially, of course—and until you go to the chair!"

Why was Fordney suspicious of Doctor Orman? Turn page for solution.

• • • • •   **$40,000 RANSOM**   • • • • •

Professor Fordney had been informed that Amos Rector would be dropped by a car half a block from his home that night. Kidnapped ten days previously, the $40,000 ransom had just been paid by Rector's brother.

Standing in the dark as a large sedan came to a stop at the intersection of Clark and Camp Streets Fordney looked at his luminous wrist watch. It was exactly 11:38 P.M.

He followed the man who left the car. Just as he was about to enter the brightly-lighted Rector home, Fordney touched the tall, slim, perfectly groomed figure on the shoulder. The man turned in alarm.

"You're Rector?" asked Fordney introducing himself.
"Yes, Professor . . . come in . . . what is it you want?"

* * *

After being greeted hysterically by his wife, they all sat in front of a cheerful fire.

"No, I don't know where I was kept," said Rector. "The kidnapers kept me blindfolded all the time until just before they released me. I had to sleep in my clothes, but they shaved me every day and gave me plenty of good food. Once, when I tried to tear off the blindfold, someone standing in back of me hit me a terrific blow on the head, knocking me unconscious."

Fordney, noticing the bump just above the right ear, asked, "When was that?"

"As nearly as I can figure, about two days ago."

"Why didn't they take that diamond ring off your finger?"

"Why . . . I . . . really don't know."

"You're lying about this matter and I want the truth!" the Professor retorted.

How did he know Rector was lying? Turn page for solution.

How did he know Rector was lying? Turn page for solution.

Solution — Death in the Cards

Had Orman fired at "the burglar" while lying on the floor, as he said, the bullet could not possibly have taken a downward course in the body—as it did.

JEALOUSY, THAT DOTES AND DOOMS, AND MURDERS, YET ADORES — Sprague

"Monday we start movin' in on the North Side," calmly announced Chuck Reardon, South Side vice and gambling czar. The cold eyes of his mobsters were expressionless.

"It'll be quite a chore," observed Tough Tommy McManus.

* * *

"Hey, Reardon!" a man in the sedan shouted. The gang leader turned. Five slugs sent him hurtling to another world.

* * *

Preliminary investigation indicated to the Professor that the Inner Circle which controlled the North Side's rackets was responsible for Reardon's murder. Because of the job's importance, Fordney thought it had been performed by one of the high command—Phil Lander, Dominick Ferraci, Alice Draper, Paul Meyerson and Tex Sterling. Further investigation disclosed the following:

1. Reardon's murderer and Phil Lander served the first of their many jail and prison terms together in Wales when both were seventeen.

2. The day before Reardon was shot his murderer learned that one of his Inner Circle companions was an epileptic. The cleverest one of the mob, this man had never been picked up by the police.

3. Reardon's killer had a beautiful moll whom he had trouble keeping in line. Despite his instructions the girl (not a mob member) needled Lander by telling Tex Sterling that Lander's wife was playing around with the man who was epileptic—though she did not know at the time he suffered the disease. She was sure the information would eventually get to Lander.

4. When Sterling told Ferraci about it, the latter advised him to have someone else tell Lander.

Despite the meagerness of the above information, study of it revealed the killer's identity to Professor Fordney.

Who is the killer? Turn page for solution.

Who is the killer? Turn page for solution.

• • •   MISTAKEN IDENTIFICATION   • • •

"I knew the body had been in water for some days, all right," said Harbor Detective Ronson, as he and Professor Fordney proceeded to the morgue where the formal identification of the remains was to take place.

"We found him where you said we probably would," continued Ronson. "A nasty sight he was, too, lying face down on the muddy river bank, the back of his head battered in and covered with blood and his clothes sodden and almost colorless as only long immersion makes them. And his face! Well you'll see that for yourself. He had been in the water for at least four days. I'm confident it's

---

Solution — $40,000 Ransom

Professor Fordney knew Rector was lying because he said he had slept in his clothes for ten days, yet when he stepped out of the car he was perfectly groomed. This evidence was offered in court and both the judge and jury found it important.

WHAT CAN GIVE US MORE SURE KNOWLEDGE THAN OUR SENSES? HOW ELSE CAN WE DISTINGUISH BETWEEN THE TRUE AND THE FALSE? — *Lucretius*

Butterworth from the description, though I couldn't make out the papers on the body."

Fordney turned a quizzical glance toward the detective as the taxi sped to the house of death, but said nothing. Arriving there they found in the outer office a tearful Mrs. Butterworth, accompanied by her brother. After a word or two with them, the deputy coroner, the Professor and the detective went to the air-cooled chamber below where an attendant pulled out a slab on which lay the green and bloated body of a man.

Mrs. Butterworth steeled herself to take a look and cried, "That's not Charles!", then fainted. Her brother definitely confirmed his sister's statement. The body was not that of Charles Butterworth.

* * *

"While a mistake in identification is understandable in such a case, I'm quite surprised at your oversight, Ronson," Fordney said later. "You should have known better!"

What did the Professor mean?

• • • • •   AN OLD RACKET   • • • • •

"You gentlemen," said Professor Fordney to members of the Bankers' Association, "must be more alert if you are to stamp out the many bank rackets that are now flourishing.

"For instance, I was standing third in line in the First National Bank yesterday morning when I noticed a man dressed in morning clothes, standing on the opposite side of the room, pick up a blotter that had just been used by a wealthy woman.

125

"While I was watching him the man in front of me had spread open his newspaper and was intently perusing it. Glancing over his shoulder I noted the headline, CHECK FORGED BY MEANS OF BLOTTER. As I was reading the article the phone in the cashier's cage rang and I heard Wilkins, to whom I always make my deposits, say in an excited

Solution — The High Command

1. Phil Lander is not the murderer.
2. The killer had a criminal record since boyhood. The epileptic had never been picked up by the police, hence the epileptic is not the killer.
3. As Reardon's killer and the epileptic were men, Alice Draper is not the murderer.
4. Dominick Ferraci is not the epileptic. As the others have been eliminated as such, Paul Meyerson is the epileptic. Hence Dominick Ferraci is the man who murdered Chuck Reardon.

I AM WEARY OF CONJECTURES; THIS MUST END THEM — Addison

Solution — Mistaken Identification

Detective Ronson told Fordney the body had been in the water at least four days. Had that been true there could not possibly have been any blood on the corpse's head. The water would obviously have washed it away during the time.

BLOOD! BAH! — Faucheur

voice, 'In the safety deposit vault? I'll take care of them immediately, Mr. Newins.'

"Apologizing to the man at the window, and calling to me, 'Be with you in a minute,' he was gone. Again I turned to watch the gentleman in the frock coat. He was still apparently studying the blotter. My curiosity was aroused, and I had just stepped out of line when the cashier returned and shouted that his cage had been robbed.

"While there were almost a hundred people there at the time, the robber would have made his getaway had I not signaled to a guard who caught him.

"It's an old trick."

"You are right, Professor," interrupted a member, "and I know how it is accomplished."

Do you? Turn page for solution.

• • • • • • **THE EYE** • • • • • • •

"Well, that's the story, Professor. I realize now that I was a fool to pay off on those first two blackmailing notes. But if I hadn't . . ." Anthony Lane shrugged dejectedly. "I did steal this money the writer accuses me of—twenty-five years ago. But I repaid every penny. And twenty years ago I made a fresh start in this state. I've worked hard and honestly and I've been fortunate. I want to serve in the Senate—but you know as well as I that if my past is exposed my political career is ended. And this appears the chief purpose of the blackmailer. Will you help me?"

Fordney would. He studied the last of the poorly spelled, illiterately scrawled blackmail letters.

Lane:

get anuther grand reddy by wensday; or else. And get out of Sennit race by then, or the peepul will no you are a cruk.

Yrs,

"The Eye"

Three days later "The Eye," Ed Morrel, walked into Fordney's trap.

* * *

The criminologist leaned back in his chair, "Morrel, comparison of these specimens of your known handwrit-

---

Solution — An Old Racket

This racket, which is often performed in metropolitan banks, is thus accomplished: The gang first learns of an important depositor having a safety deposit box. The timing is carefully done so that just as the inside member arrives at the cashier's cage the cashier is telephoned by an outside member (from an adjacent drugstore or similar place) stating that he is the depositor who has just remembered he left some bonds on a shelf in the vault and requests the cashier to take care of them immediately.

The cashier naturally agrees to do so and hurries away. While the second man in line opens his newspaper, thus hiding his confederate, the man at the cage extracts the money and walks out! The man in the morning suit is a decoy.

IF MANY GO BEFORE, ALL WAYS DO LIE OPEN — *Shakespeare*

---

ing with these blackmail threats, proves you wrote both. Well?"

Relief showed on Lane's face.

"Yeah, I wrote 'em,—so what?" challenged Morrel. "This is a free country, ain't it? I don't want no crook representin' me, so ain't I got a right to say so? And if the chump wants to kick through with a couple of grand, that's his business, mister—and mine. See?"

Fordney bulleted the question. "Who is your accomplice, Morrel?"

"Nobody. I'm doin' this strictly solo, mister."

"That," said the Professor, "is a lie! You wrote those notes, yes, but you copied them. Who wrote the originals?"

Why did Fordney believe Morrel had an accomplice? Turn page for solution.

• • • • • • CLASS DAY • • • • • •

"On picking up the Daily Herald this morning," said Professor Fordney to his class in criminology, "I was really amazed to read in bold headlines that John Stevens and members of his gang had been caught after a daring bank robbery by Herman Schlitz, an ex-member of our class.

"I thought Stevens had gone straight after I helped him out of the last trouble he was in. That I didn't keep tabs on him is one on your old Prof. At the head of column ten, where the story was continued from the front page, there was a picture of Stevens that I would never have recognized. The paper stated that his altered appearance was due to plastic surgery, so I can't really blame myself too much, although I should have recognized those eyes . . . but then my alibi is that the wired photograph was rather poor!

129

"It was gratifying to know that one of my pupils was responsible for the arrest and that he showed not only great detective ability, but extreme courage in effecting it. I hope all you lads, when called upon, will rise to an occasion as well," he continued.

"The peculiar thing is that Stevens had always been a lone wolf and I find it difficult to understand why he, this time, worked as leader of a gang. However, despite Cesare Lombroso's theory, human nature, criminal or otherwise, can never be definitely cataloged. I . . . what's that . . ."

"Only this, Professor," said Bob Wilkerson, jumping up excitedly. "I know that yarn of yours isn't true. You won't catch me any more!"

What was wrong with the Professor's story? Turn page for solution.

Usually the Professor gave little heed to anonymous letters. But this one, threatening his life, angered him. It was a particularly vicious and cold-blooded letter. He decided it was from the shadowy but ruthless Velvet Glove mob which had recently moved in with violence and bloodshed, and had taken over the rackets from the notorious McMann gang.

The mob was large, with many ramifications, but the criminologist learned that the four who controlled it were Alvin Fonda, Rex Stover, Joe Martineau and Ralph Coburn. One of them was a foreigner illegally in the country. Intensive investigation revealed the following:

a. In a gambling joint, flushed with liquor and large winnings, Joe Martineau shouted that he and the syndicate's leader, nicknamed Deadly, had recently killed Sheriff Tom Murdock, whose murder remained unsolved.

b. When Fonda learned of this he was furious and told the gang member who acted as treasurer to let Deadly know that Martineau was getting out of line.

c. Informed of Fonda's action, Martineau laughed and told Ralph Coburn that a little thing like that wouldn't annoy Deadly. Besides Deadly was pretty proud of the job and not above boasting of it himself.

d. The foreigner, who was left-handed, was opposed to sending Fordney the threatening letter. Deadly, the treasurer and Fonda, however, insisted. They maintained that regardless of its effect upon the Professor, its publication would whip into line some others who were being troublesome.

From the above Fordney determined identities of the leader, the treasurer, and foreigner—and went to work.

Who is the foreigner? The treasurer? The leader? Turn page for solution.

• • •   **MURDER IN THE GARDEN**   • • •

The only marks on the body were deep bruises made by powerful fingers on the beautiful white throat. Strangled. The Professor was baffled.

It seemed such a senseless crime! Who could have killed this charming, unsophisticated girl only a month out of a convent? A thorough probing failed to disclose the slightest motive. Fordney had come to the conclusion it was the work of a homicidal maniac, when Sergeant Reynolds pushed Hip Ling, the family cook, into the room.

"The chauffeur says he saw this Chink lurking in the garden just before the girl was murdered last night. I'm going to take his prints and see if we have them at headquarters."

As the Chinaman's hand was pressed to the pad, Fordney observed the man's lithe strength, the long-nailed, powerful fingers, the unusual reach of the arms. He also noticed he was left-handed. The traditional imperturbabil-

---

Solution — Class Day

No daily newspaper in the United States has ten columns. The Professor was again trying to test his students' observational powers of the commonplace.

THE CAREFUL READER OF A FEW GOOD NEWSPAPERS CAN LEARN MORE IN A YEAR THAN MOST SCHOLARS DO IN THEIR GREAT LIBRARIES — *Sanborn*

ity of the Oriental, however, was lacking. Here was a badly frightened, greatly excited, wildly gesticulating Chinaman!

Loudly Hip Ling proclaimed his innocence. He admitted being in the garden waiting to meet a smuggler who had agreed to bring his brother into the country. Nothing could induce him, however, to name this man. Fear of the tongs, he said. When he stated he had seen no one but Miss Hazel, who for a long time, stood silently staring up at the stars, Reynolds let out a yell and slapped the cuffs on him.

"You don't believe him, eh, Sergeant?" inquired Fordney. "Well, stars were shining last night. No, Ling didn't murder the girl!"

How did Fordney know? Turn page for solution.

• • • ... AND READ THE PAGE • • •

Prasilov, famed, fabulous Polish astrologer lay dead on the floor of the observation room in the ancient stone tower in Cornwall, England. Shot through the right temple, his massive head rested on a huge book of astrological charts, opened at his own horoscope! Death had been instantaneous. A revolver of foreign make lay a few feet distant.

Fordney and Chief Inspector Tarwheel puffed up the long flight of stone steps.

"The door was locked, sir. We had to force it," explained Constable Stibble.

The chief inspector picked up a key lying near the body, looked inquiringly at Stibble.

"That's where it was, sir. I've disturbed nothing."

Had Prasilov locked himself in and dropped the key there hoping to confuse or baffle the police? Had it fallen from the lock when the door was forced, or was there another explanation? The Professor wondered.

The body removed, Fordney lifted the massive book and studied the seer's horoscope. There was a small amount of blood where his head had rested. Peering over Fordney's shoulder, Tarwheel read the prediction on that date of the noted astrologer's death by suicide!

"Something queer here, Professor," the chief inspector observed. "But"—he frowned—"what could it be but suicide?"

Solution — Anonymous

Joe Martineau is not the leader, Deadly (a), or (b) the treasurer. Alvin Fonda (b) is neither treasurer nor leader. Ralph Coburn (c) is not the leader, hence the leader, known as Deadly, is Rex Stover. And, as the leader is not the treasurer, we see in (b) that Coburn is the treasurer. Therefore, as neither the leader (Stover), the treasurer (Coburn), nor Fonda (d) is the foreigner, he is Joe Martineau.

Solution — Murder in the Garden

As the only marks on the girl's throat were bruises, Fordney knew the Chinaman did not strangle her. Had he done so, his long nails would have left scratches.

LEND THY SERIOUS HEARING TO WHAT I SHALL UNFOLD — Shakespeare

"Murder," said Fordney.

Fifteen minutes later, from halfway down the stone steps, Tarwheel called a bit impatiently: "Coming, Professor?"

The astrological book under his arm, Fordney took a last look around. Blood on the floor previously hidden by the book was the only remaining evidence of the tragedy.

"Coming," he answered. Didn't Tarwheel know it was murder?

What clue proved not suicide but murder? Turn page for solution.

• • • • **LIGHT ON THE SUBJECT** • • • •

"You will stand at the door and if he . . . You understand, Suzette?"

"Oui, Madame," replied the chic maid.

* * *

"Please, Anthony, do let's return to town," pleaded Ethel Warfield. "I simply cannot stand this gloomy old house in the country any longer. Ugh . . . it gives me the creeps."

Convalescent Anthony Warfield said: "No, my dear,— you loved this old house before we were married. But now you find it intolerable to remain away from your café society 'friends' for a few months even when you know what the country means to me. I . . ."

There was a knock. Suzette entered.

"Pardon, Madame. Your other riding habit—I cannot locate it."

"It's in the attic," Ethel told her. "Please get it."

* * *

What a tragedy, thought Fordney, that this once lovely

old country house should now be a mass of fire-gutted wreckage.

"Yes, Monsieur?" The maid had quietly entered the summer house.

The Professor crossed his legs. "Tell me about it, Suzette."

"There is not much. Madame wants her riding habit from the attic. It is old and musty there. My flashlight it fails so I use my cigarette lighter to look about. Suddenly one of those old giant cobwebs caught fire. The flames shot out and ignited some old papers. In a moment —puff!—the attic was on fire."

"You," said Fordney observing the girl's hair, "were fortunate in escaping."

"My luck, she is always good," smiled the petite maid.

Fordney shook his head. "This time, the Lady has deserted you, Suzette. Arson will be the charge!"

Why? Turn page for solution.

Solution — . . . And Read the Page

Blood under the book proved Prasilov was murdered. Had he been a suicide from an instantly fatal wound, there could not have been blood under the massive book. His murderer (a servant) possessed a key to the tower room. After killing the astrologer, he took Prasilov's key from his pocket, dropped it on the floor, then locked the door from the outside with his key which he took with him.

I WILL LOOK ON THE STARS AND LOOK ON THEE, AND READ THE PAGE OF THY DESTINY — Landon

"Observation of the commonplace—conscious notice of those things which we see almost every day but which most of us do not observe—this faculty, gentlemen, you must develop." Fordney was addressing a group of West Coast air raid wardens during the war.

"Let me illustrate. Hearing a cry from an office building, an air raid warden located a dying man in a third floor office. Blood was spurting from several knife wounds. Calling an ambulance he turned to the janitor.

" 'What do you know about this?' he demanded.

" 'Not much. As I was cleaning the hall I noticed fresh blood on the hinges of Mr. Dawson's door here, so I tried the door. It was unlocked. I pushed it open a few inches and saw him lying there by the desk.'

" 'Was the light on?'

" 'Yes—and the shades were drawn.'

" 'See anybody leave this office tonight?' the warden queried, noting the top desk drawer was open.

" 'Saw a woman walking down the hall about ten minutes ago but I don't know which office she came from.'

"The air raid warden," Fordney continued, "looked intently at the janitor.

" 'Touch anything in here?'

" 'No.'

"The warden stepped out into the hall. He noted the janitor's pail, mop, wringer and wash cloth—the latter showing indications of blood. The warden noted many things but failed to observe the single, commonplace thing (or recall it to his mind) which would have told him immediately the janitor was lying."

What was it? Turn page for solution.

Professor Fordney and his host, Sheriff Tom Brennan, sat over after-breakfast coffee.

"This mob, Professor, is going to drive me out of my mind," the sheriff said. "They escape on motorcycles, meet at a predetermined rendezvous, abandon their cycles and continue in a souped-up car. They killed three men in my county last week. We've got to get them, Fordney!"

"Who comprises the gang?" the criminologist asked.

"Pierre Meget, Axel Drew, Ernst Krause and Tom Reardon. The only other information I've been able to pick up is this:

"A. Drew's sister and the leader's cousin are ex-shop-lifters. One of the four is an expert mechanic who keeps the mob's transportation in excellent condition. This man's sister is the leader's sweetheart.

Solution — Light on the Subject

Cobwebs do not flame.

**THE MOST TANGIBLE OF ALL VISIBLE MYSTERIES —
FIRE — Leigh Hunt**

Solution — Alert for the Air Raid Wardens

The warden failed to observe that there were no hinges on the outside of Dawson's office. He completely overlooked the fact that hinges of doors which open inwardly are on the inside.

ABSURDITY REFUTES ITSELF — Bartholin

B. Although he wears glasses, Pierre Meget and the mechanic boast that Tom Reardon is the finest pistol shot in the world.

C. Several days ago, Reardon brought two Chicago hoods to the gang's temporary hideout and suggested to the leader and the mechanic that they become mob members. The leader turned down the suggestion.

"That's all I have, Prof. Who do you think is the mob's leader?"

Fordney smiled. "That's easy, Tom. The leader is . . . . Therefore, the mechanic who plays such an important part in these crimes is . . . ."

Who is the leader? Who is the mechanic? Turn page for solution.

• • • • • **A SOUND SLEEPER** • • • • •

Professor Fordney's attention was attracted by a suspicious-looking bulge in the right pocket of an obviously expensive camel's hair overcoat which was thrown carelessly over Skamp's green coat.

"That yours?" he asked John London.

"Yes, sir. You see . . ."

"Just a moment," interrupted the Professor. A rather sheepish grin spread over his face when he found the bulge in the coat was made by a large peppermint candy cane. Examining the green coat, a sudden thought struck him. Perhaps that cane did have some significance!

He had already seen the body of Henry Skamp lying on the floor of the one-room apartment. Skamp had been stabbed.

"All right," Fordney nodded to London, "continue."

"Last night Henry came home a bit drunk, woke me up, and when I refused to listen to him tell about his love affair he flung his coat on that chair and lay down beside me fully dressed. I was tired and went right back to sleep. When I awoke this morning—around 9 o'clock—I found him lying there dead and called the police."

"You heard no sound after you went to sleep the second time and you disturbed nothing?" the Professor inquired.

"No—I was dead tired."

"How long have you two been roommates?"

"Oh, quite a while."

"How long?"

"About two years. I forgot to tell you that three months ago Henry lost his job and he's been brooding ever since."

"H'mmmm . . .!" Fordney pondered a moment. "You're lying, London. I'm holding you on suspicion!"

Why? Turn page for solution.

Solution — The Mob

a. We see that the leader is not the mechanic. Also that Axel Drew is neither leader nor mechanic.

b. Pierre Meget is neither the mechanic nor the expert shot.

c. Tom Reardon is not the leader nor is he the mechanic. Hence, Axel Drew is eliminated as leader, mechanic or expert shot. Therefore, as Pierre Meget is not the mechanic, he is the mob's leader. This leaves Ernst Krause as the expert mechanic.

For some days considerable mystery surrounded the emergency landing of Otto Freund and Ernst Wagner in a single-motored plane near an Army post at 11:05 P.M. two nights before the Pearl Harbor atrocity.

With a group of Army officers and War Department officials, Professor Fordney was observing a demonstration of the latest development in anti-aircraft searchlights. Mounted on an Army truck in a camp field the searchlight was shooting its infrared beam more than fourteen miles into the sky when suddenly a plane roared out of the starless night and with a sputtering roar landed in a rough field a few hundred yards distant.

One of the plane's occupants, Ernst Wagner, was dead, the other, pilot Otto Freund, only slightly injured. Freund bitterly blamed his crash landing and Wagner's death on the Army demonstration.

A check of the plane's instruments was made without results, as they were badly damaged.

"How," the Professor asked after Freund's tirade ended, "did you get nine miles off your course?"

"How! How!" the excited pilot exclaimed. "Because I mistook the beam of your searchlight for an emergency landing field just after my motor began acting up. Naturally I headed for your light instead of trying to keep on my course. If only I had tried to maintain my course I would have made the emergency field at Oakdale."

Fordney stared into the moonless night, turned his collar up against the biting west wind. He nodded to the commanding officer who barked: "Take this spying liar to the guardhouse, Sergeant!"

Why did Fordney and the officer disbelieve Freund's account? Why did they suspect him of espionage? A single clue, which the well-informed should know, answers both questions. Turn page for solution.

• • •   **FORDNEY IS INCENSED**   • • • •

Old Rachel hummed a plaintive spiritual as she put on her stiff, freshly starched petticoats—no self-respecting colored mammy would wear less than two—slipped on a huge red dress and surveyed her lugubrious self in the mirror. She had misery of de spirit. Well, maybe Miz Morgan would . . .

Rachel went downstairs.

* * *

"From the top step I saw Rachel standing in the hall looking furtively about," said Ronald Morgan. "She must have heard me when I started down because she ran to the telephone and began hollering, 'Police! Police!' into the transmitter. I . . ."

"But you know how excited she gets, Ronald," wealthy Mrs. Muriel Morgan reminded her nephew. "No one be-

---

Solution — A Sound Sleeper

London said he was asleep when Skamp came in and flung his coat on the chair, and that he had disturbed nothing. As Professor Fordney found London's coat on top of Skamp's he knew, of course, that London was lying.

MINDS THAT HAVE NOTHING TO CONFER FIND LITTLE TO PERCEIVE — *Wordsworth*

lieves, Professor, that Rachel hit me over the head and robbed my safe."

"But," said Fordney, "someone who knew the position and combination of the safe did both. And you three were alone."

"But the house was wide open, Joe," Muriel Morgan protested. "Anyone could have come in unobserved."

"Perhaps. But 'anyone' wouldn't have known the safe combination. Did Rachel know it?"

"Why, yes. She's seen me open it a hundred times."

As the tearful Rachel ambled across the living room toward them Fordney asked: "Didn't you hear anything, Muriel?"

"No, I didn't. I was sitting here in the sun parlor knitting. There was utter silence. Suddenly someone hit me on the back of the head."

The Professor stared at the thick, pile carpet on the living room and sun-parlor floor, said scathingly: "Ronald is not only guilty of theft but of a subtle and abominable attempt to frame your old servant!"

How did Fordney know that Rachel was innocent? Turn page for solution.

• • • • • •   CLASS DAY   • • • • • •

"I had dinner with an old friend of mine last evening," said Professor Fordney to his class at the University. "He related some of his interesting experiences as a young missionary in Africa, and one incident impressed me as being peculiarly applicable to our purpose. As the criminal investigator is frequently called upon to meet odd and unusual circumstances and as this story illustrates the successful handling of a perplexing situation, I am going to give it to you as your problem for today.

"Three missionaries were taking three cannibals to missionary headquarters. By themselves, or with an equal number of whites, the cannibals were entirely tractable. At the slightest opportunity, however, the missionaries knew they would revert to cannibalism. Therefore, it was

---

Solution — Fordney Sees the Light

When Otto Freund said he mistook the beam of the anti-aircraft searchlight and headed for its light, the Professor knew he was lying, because an infrared beam of light is invisible to the human eye! One could stare into an infrared searchlight which is throwing its beam miles into the sky, and see only blackness.

This type of searchlight records any object on which it falls on special photographic plates, thus enabling anti-aircraft guns to be trained on planes the infrared beam picks out.

I NEVER SAW AN EYE SO BRIGHT — Mrs. Welby

Solution — Fordney Is Incensed

When Fordney heard the rustle of Rachel's starched petticoats as she ambled across the living room, he knew it would have been impossible for her to have crossed the sun parlor, unheard by Mrs. Morgan. Also he knew the thick pile carpet would have deadened Ronald's steps. Ronald confessed.

KNAVERY ADDS MALICE TO FALSEHOOD — Bruyere

absolutely necessary that at all times there should be no more cannibals than missionaries together.

"Preparing to cross a river, they found that their small boat would hold only two people. None of them could swim and while all the missionaries could row, only one of the cannibals could. What a dilemma!

"After some thought one of the missionaries arrived at the manner of getting across without permitting there to be at any time more cannibals than missionaries on the same side of the river. Oh yes, the cannibal who could row was named Whatso!

"Yes, you may use matches, pencils or anything you like to represent the cannibals and missionaries. Hop to it, fellows," concluded the Professor with a smile.

How did you get them across? Turn page for solution.

• • • • • • • ROUND-UP • • • • • • • •

"Heard you rounded up the Four Aces mob," said Tom Howard, sinking into a chair in the Professor's study. "Nice work. Tell me about it."

"Not much to it, really," replied Fordney.

"Don't be so modest. Give," commanded the criminologist's old friend.

"Delighted." Fordney lit a cigar. "The Four Aces," he said, "are Avis Monroe, Dick Graver, Al Toliver and Lou Jackson.

(1) "Saturday night I followed them, in slight disguise, to Ox Burkam's notorious nightclub. The four had a drink and the gang leader left. Shortly afterwards Lou Jackson and the mob's front went to another table and drank champagne with two businessmen. When the leader returned he was informed of this, smacked

the lovely Lou in the face, and accused her of setting up a private shakedown.

(2) Later I heard the leader tell Avis Monroe he'd break Lou's jaw if she tried anything on her own.

(3) Suddenly Al Toliver and the front spotted me. The lights went out. The four escaped. But later that night Sergeant Bill Jopke and I closed in on Avis and her mob boy friend at the Amazon. Sunday I received a tip that the other two mobsters were at the Hotel Minerva. I went down and got 'em."

"That's all?" asked Howard.

(4) "Yes, except I forgot to mention that the leader has black hair, the front is blond and Dick Graver's eyes are blue. And so," chuckled Fordney, "you now know, of course, who the leader is and who is the front."

Solution — Class Day

1. Cannibal, missionary row across.
2. Missionary rows back.
3. Whatso, cannibal row over.
4. Whatso rows back.
5. Two missionaries row across.
6. Missionary, cannibal row back.
7. Whatso, missionary row across.
8. Missionary, cannibal row back.
9. Two missionaries row over.
10. Whatso rows back, returns with one cannibal, rows back again bringing other cannibal across.

O YE GODS! WHAT THICK ENCIRCLING DARKNESS BLINDS THE MINDS OF MEN — Ovid

Tom Howard blinked and reached for his drink.

Who is the leader? Who is the front? Turn page for solution.

Turn page for solution.

• • • HE WHO PLAYS WITH FIRE • • •

Sheriff Tom Bronson's chair creaked as he teetered back, locked fingers behind his head. Professor Fordney fired a cigar. The office clock struck eleven.

"Go on," said Bronson.

"Wally Gregg and I were alone at Hobson's boat house this afternoon,—about 2:30 it was." Frank Dane wet his lips and continued. "We got into an argument over a girl and he knocked me into the water. I swam out to the float —Gregg can't swim—and when he left, swam back, got my boat and rowed up river to fish."

"In these clothes?"

"Yes. It was dark when I returned. On the path from the boat house to the road I stumbled over Gregg's dead body. I . . ."

"Hold it!" snapped Bronson. "If it was dark how did you know it was Gregg's body?"

"I struck one of these." Dane held out a folder of safety matches.

"Have those on you when Gregg shoved you in?" Bronson asked.

"Yes."

"That's all!" barked Bronson. "Those matches would still have been wet and you can't light wet matches!"

"But they weren't wet, Sheriff. I dried them in the sun with my clothes." The suspect smirked.

"We didn't find any burned matches near the body," Fordney said.

"I wasn't taking any chances of being framed so I put the burned stubs in my pocket. Here they are. See?"

The Professor looked at the ceiling. Bronson frowned. "Lock him up, Sheriff. He's lying. A cunning man is generally a fool."

What obvious lie caused Dane's arrest? Turn page for solution.

• • • • • • **CASE NO. 299** • • • • • •

MIDNIGHT: Collar turned up, the Professor tramped through the driving rain of the gusty night with a feeling of exhilaration. Bracing! That's what it was. He'd just broken the baffling Holman case.

1 A.M.: Home.

1:30 A.M.: In dressing gown and slippers reading before a blazing fire.

2 A.M.: Roughead's, *The Murderer's Companion,* slipped to the floor. Fordney was asleep. The blasting wind howled an eerie accompaniment to his stentorian breathing.

Solution — Round-Up

It is apparent in (1) that Lou Jackson is neither leader nor front. In (2) we see that Avis Monroe is not the leader. Obviously (3) Al Toliver is not the gang's front. From (4) it is clear that Dick Graver is not the leader or the front. Consequently Al Toliver is the gang leader and Avis Monroe the front.

REASON CAN DISCOVER THINGS — *Quarles*

---

4 A.M.: Telephone bell ringing shrilly. A sleepy, grouchy, "Hello?" An irritable, "All right." What a life!

4:30 A.M.: Driving through clear, gray dawn. Heater out of commission. Damn such weather! Man might catch his death of cold! A shiver. Gad, what a terrible cigar!

4:55 A.M.: Body of actor Eric Hendrick slumped against arm of park bench. Ill-fitting top hat perched on side of massive head above handsome features set in ghastly grimace. Cast of characters: Inspector Kelley; Doctor Winslow; cops; dicks; driver. Props: squad cars; morgue wagon.

WINSLOW: "Hendrick was killed between 12 an 1:30. Shot twice."

KELLEY: "What in hell was he sittin' on a bench in the rain at that hour for? Must have been bumped by somebody he knew. But why?" Kelley popped two jujubes into his mouth.

6:30 A.M.: Home. Fordney's housekeeper hovering solicitously.

FORDNEY: "Delicious pancakes, these, Mary!" If any bloodstains on bench, rain washed them away. Hendrick's famous walking-stick. Where was it? H'mmmm ... might be a lead. "Another cup of coffee, please." Kelley's job to learn where Hendrick was killed. I told him he wasn't murdered where found. Ah! Wonderful cigar, this!

How did the Professor know Hendrick had not been killed where found? Turn page for solution.

149

"What in the name of God are you doing?" The words snapped like a volley through the still, cold air of the north woods.

* * *

Kneeling on the hard trail Fordney carefully removed Fred Thompson's hunting knife from his heart. He broke the deer rifles of the two men standing near. Both were loaded.

* * *

The Professor put down his power glass. "Yours," he said, "are the only fingerprints on the smooth handle of Thompson's hunting knife."

"But I told you, Fordney, how they got there!" exclaimed Orville Hodge. "You've got to believe me! I . . ."

"Let's have your account again, Almy," the Professor interrupted.

Solution — *He Who Plays with Fire*

Once safety matches are wet, they will not light even though dried.

CUNNING IS THE DWARF OF REASON — *Alger*

Solution — *Case No. 299*

Hendrick was killed between 12 and 1:30 while there was a gusty storm, yet his ill-fitting opera hat was perched on the side of his massive head! Had he been killed on the bench, the wind would have blown the hat from his head.

WHILE ROCKING WINDS ARE PIPING LOUD — *Milton*

"About four o'clock I headed back toward our cabin—we were hunting separately. As I came up the trail I saw Orville bending over Fred as though he were pushing that knife into him. I hollered and he jumped to his feet!"

"I found Fred with that knife in him!" Hodge protested. "I thought perhaps he was living and that if I pulled the knife out it would help. Then I saw he was dead and just as Jim hollered I remembered that nothing should be touched."

Fordney again interrupted. "No one but you three were in the area. You had just shot a deer, Hodge, and were returning for help to clean it—yet I found your gun fully loaded!"

"I . . . I . . . had exhausted the ammunition in the gun when I shot the deer and, not knowing whether it was dead, re-loaded before I approached it."

"Quite. Don't move," the criminologist said as he covered Thompson's murderer.

Whom did Fordney arrest for Thompson's murder? Why? Turn page for solution.

• • • •   THE STOLEN FORMULA   • • • •

"I had just stepped behind that screen near the door to wash my hands when a man, gun in hand, entered the room and stood motionless for a few seconds," said Ryder. "Apparently satisfied that no one was here, he walked to the desk over there by the window. As he rummaged through the papers in the drawer, I hastily dialed Police 1313, leaving the receiver off the hook, trusting you would trace the call. I was afraid to talk because I was unarmed and he looked like a desperate fellow."

"You say he took nothing from your desk but a valuable formula?" Fordney looked skeptical.

"That's all."

"Rather careless to leave such an important paper lying about like that, wasn't it?"

"Well I suppose so, though it was only a copy. I sold the original to Fuller yesterday for $20,000 and I intended destroying the duplicate tonight."

"Would that formula be valuable to anyone else?"

"Yes. It would be worth twice as much to the Mason Company."

"Why didn't you sell it to them in the first place?"

"Fuller financed me while I was perfecting it—I had to

Solution — Fate on the Trail

As Orville Hodge's were the only fingerprints on Thompson's hunting knife (with which he was stabbed) this was proof of Hodge's innocence; proof that someone had wiped the knife handle after stabbing Thompson and before Hodge touched it. Had Thompson been a suicide his prints would have been on the knife. If Hodge were the murderer he would not have senselessly wiped the knife clean then deliberately accused himself by putting his prints on it again. Thus, Fordney knew that, as the three men were alone in the area, Jim Almy murdered Thompson and wiped the knife clean to remove his prints. He was unwisely elated when he saw Hodge with his hand on the knife for he was hanged for his crime.

BUT, O VAIN BOAST WHO CAN CONTROL HIS FATE — *Shakespeare*

sell to him—even though I could have got more from Mason."

"As this is such a small, bright room and you observed so much through that crack in the screen, you should be able to give a VERY good description of the intruder."

"Oh, I can do that," Ryder replied with assurance. "He was a small man—about 125 pounds—blond hair, light complexion and unusually large nose and vicious-looking mouth. As he left, obviously unaware of my presence, I noticed he had a big rip in the back of his blue coat."

"Well, Ryder, as part of your story is untrue, you can't expect me to believe any of it!"

Why did the Professor suspect Ryder? Turn page for solution.

• • • • THE MOTH GETS SINGED • • • •

Beauteous, thrill-seeking debutante Lorna Waring was aglow with excitement. She had met some real crooks and killers and they had talked openly before her! Lorna was ecstatic. This sinister mob, well-dressed and well-mannered, was composed of Bebe Held, Alice Avon, Tex Logan, Loren Northrup and Hank Jessing.

Quite by accident Lorna witnessed a stick-up by two of the mob. She pledged undying secrecy. But the mob wasn't buying. She was invited to participate in a daring jewel robbery. She refused. The next day Lorna was in the morgue.

The above is what Professor Fordney knew when he started out to round up the vicious gang. It was not long before he had the following information:

1. One of the mob was a highly gifted bridge player. He had excellent social contacts.

2. Loren Northrup, one-time croupier, had evolved a neat gambling racket and tried to enlist the cooperation of the bridge expert. Disliking Northrup, the bridge player refused.

3. Though Hank Jessing and the bridge player hated and distrusted each other they worked smoothly together in mob business.

4. Bebe Held told a friend that the gang member who actually shot Lorna Waring to death did so as much in wild jealousy as fear of her knowledge of gang affairs. Bebe added that the bridge expert, also infatuated with Lorna, had pleaded with the murderer, who was a close friend, not to kill the society girl.

Although this was all Fordney had to work on, he and picked homicide detectives had the entire mob in custody in less than a week.

Who murdered Lorna Waring? Turn page for solution.

Solution — The Stolen Formula

In a small room the intruder would have heard Ryder dialing headquarters and therefore could not have been unaware of his presence. As Ryder had obviously lied about this, Fordney was convinced he had fabricated the entire story in order to sell the formula twice.

DON'T TELL ME OF DECEPTION; A LIE IS A LIE; WHETHER IT BE A LIE TO THE EYE OR A LIE TO THE EAR — *Dr. Johnson*

Brushing his hand across the screen, the Professor nicked his forefinger on the sharp protruding wires around the bullet hole, stepped gingerly from the plank in the flower bed on the east side of the house to the gravel walk and re-entered the house.

From the position of her body it was obvious that the maid, dainty Arvonne Dupre, had hit her head on the buffet in slumping to the floor. A single shot in the back, as she stood in direct line with the window of the huge dining room, had pierced the heart. Doctor Caldwell probed for the bullet.

"I was having a few guests for dinner—my wife's in town," Sidney Blake, owner of the country house explained. "Arvonne—the only maid we have left—you know the situation—must have been setting the table. I happened to look out of my room directly over this and saw a man, partially hidden by a tree, aim for the dining room and fire—a revolver, I think. I rushed down and found Arvonne."

Fordney faced the buffet—on which were scattered knives and forks—his back to the window 20 feet distant. He turned, walked slowly to the table, examined the place nearest the center of the large window. The cloth was slightly rumpled. On the floor was a thorny rose stem.

"I've got it," said Doctor Caldwell. ".38 caliber."

As Fordney faced the window, Blake shouted, "Look out! There he is again!" The Professor waved and the detective pointing an automatic behind a tree saluted and vanished.

"You, Blake," said the criminologist, "are under arrest for murder."

What clue broke the case for Fordney? Turn page for solution.

Sergeant Cargo picked the bottle from the floor of Homer Hudera's studio, removed the cork, sniffed its contents gingerly and handed it to Fordney.

The Professor held it absently as he continued to study the position of nineteen-year-old artist's model Eve Yardley's body on the floor. Her lips were slightly drawn back. Dressed in street clothes, she lay on her side, her right knee almost under her chin, the right forefinger of her otherwise fisted hand pointed stiffly. Her nearby handbag contained the usual miscellany—except lip rouge, though her lips were scarlet.

Solution — The Moth Gets Singed

The bridge expert (2) is not Loren Northrup.

As the bridge player (3) also is not Hank Jessing, he is Tex Logan.

Bebe Held (4) did not kill Lorna. As the bridge expert (Tex Logan) pleaded with the killer, who was a good friend, the murderer is not Northrup or Jessing (2 and 3), hence the killer is Alice Avon.

SUBJECT THYSELF TO REASON — Seneca

Solution — Death Sets the Table

Blake said the shot was fired from outside the house, yet the wire about the hole in the screen pointed outward, proving the shot went through it from the dining room. Blake paid for his dalliance with the pert little maid with his life.

TRUTH IS ALWAYS PRESENT — Emerson

Fordney smelled of the bottle and recognized one of the speediest, most powerful of poisons.

"Got her instantly," he said as he continued to rummage through her bag. "How did it happen, Hudera?"

The handsome, cynical young artist pinched out his cigarette, said:

"I gave a small studio party this afternoon. Eve was not invited but came anyway. She used to model for me but I could no longer stand her emotional outbursts. All the others left at 8 o'clock but Eve refused to go. She asked her usual question and I told her flatly I would not marry her.

"Suddenly she whipped that bottle from her bag and drank from it before I could stop her. She dropped as though shot. I . . ."

"Did you touch her bag?"

"No, I touched nothing—obviously she was dead."

With a startling snap the Professor closed Eve's bag, motioned to Cargo. "Put this cold-blooded killer where he belongs!" he ordered.

What single clue caused his action? Turn page for solution.

• • • • **A WORD TO THE WISE** • • • •

"I ain't no doctor, Tom Naby, but you got a concussion of the brain. Maybe even a little fracture of the skull. Whatever it is, you need good attention and you can't git that this side of Moorestown. I been a thinkin'. Branch line train—won't be more'n two, three people on it—leaves in two hours. That'll give me time, and you can hold out that long. Just do what I tell you now and you won't get hurt no worse'n you are. And you'll git the best hospital care—free! Besides, you'll collect a couple of hundred dollars—which you'n me'll split." Farmer Amos Sneed was right proud of himself.

* * *

Professor Fordney was almost thrown from his seat as the speeding train emergency-braked to a sudden, jolting stop. He was quite thoroughly shaken up. He looked back from his front seat to see if the grimy coach's only other passenger, whom he'd seen standing near the rear a moment before, was all right. He wasn't. Hurrying to the back of the coach, the Professor found the man sprawled on his back, apparently unconscious.

"Is he hurt much?" the anxious conductor asked a few minutes later.

"Difficult to say," Fordney replied. "He'll have to get to a hospital as quickly as possible though. What happened?"

"Hit a cow—bad light—just getting dusk. Our third accident in two months. We'll catch it from headquarters when this man puts in his claim—if he lives."

"Dusk . . . dusk," Fordney repeated. "Quite. You

Solution — No Model for Murder

Hudera said he touched nothing. Death was instantaneous —yet the cork was in the bottle! When his mistake was pointed out, the artist confessed he poisoned Eve's drink and put the bottle containing the remainder of the poison beside her; concocted his simple story and called the police. He admitted he didn't think of the cork one way or the other— it was just a natural action to put it in the bottle. It hanged him.

AN ARTIST SHOULD HAVE MORE THAN TWO EYES — *Lamartine*

needn't worry about this man's claim," he assured the conductor. "He won't make one—not if he is wise."

Why did Fordney say so? Turn page for solution.

• • • • • • • **CLASS DAY** • • • • • • •

Professor Fordney picked up a typewritten sheet from his desk and read the following to his class in criminology:

"I never expected to get back alive. The weather was cold and clear when Frank Hayes and I left for our base camp on the Arctic Circle on the morning of September 8, 1932. Three days later, on the 11th, an icy, howling wind came up as we set out . . . the worst I've ever seen. We had gone not more than two miles when Hayes took a terrific fall and was blown along the jagged ice for some distance. I managed to get him on the sled, but he knew he was fatally injured and hadn't long to live. Knowing how much in sympathy I am with his scientific theories, he said he wanted to make a will, leaving his fortune to me so I might carry on his work. I tried to dissuade him but, taking some paper and a fountain pen from his kit, he insisted I write at his dictation. He signed it and in less than an hour he was dead.

"I had to shoot two of the dogs that had been injured. All the others, but one, got away so it was impossible for me to get the body back. The wind died down shortly after Frank passed on.

"(signed) Joseph Dennis."

Fordney put down the letter and said, "I want you to tell me whether you accept this story as true . . . and why. Quickly now!"

Do you? Why? Turn page for solution.

The savagely battered body of a beautiful brown-eyed girl was discovered on the shore of a small lake in northern Wisconsin by a fisherman.

Vacationing in the area, Professor Fordney interested himself in the affair. There was no clue to the identity of the dead girl except a piece of torn envelope fifty yards from the body with the words, "Calico Dale."

The Professor's investigation disclosed that Calico Dale was a farm twenty miles away, taken over six months earlier by four girls who raised herbs and squabs. The four were Sylvia Lane, Bernice Sloan, Myra Bubley, and Carmen Marzoni. One of them, known as Dixie, answered the description of the murdered girl.

Solution — A Word to the Wise

Fordney knew that had the man been thrown to the floor by the sudden stopping of the speeding train, he would have been thrown on his face, not on his back, as found. P. S. Tom paid his own hospital bill. Amos Sneed lost a cow.

Solution — Class Day

The story was, of course, untrue. The ink in the fountain pen would have been frozen.

WINTER DOES NOT WORK ONLY ON A BROAD SCALE; HE IS CAREFUL IN TRIFLES — Smith

Fordney found the farm deserted, but from various sources pieced together the following meager information:

1. The girl who leased the farm had blue eyes, the other three had brown eyes.
2. The blue-eyed girl, a Minnesotan, and Myra Bubley and Carmen Marzoni came to the farm by train. Sylvia Lane, who had never before been in the midwest, arrived in a rented plane.
3. One of the four is an amateur hypnotist.
4. The night before they deserted the farm Sylvia Lane and the dead girl induced the hypnotist to hypnotize the latter.
5. Carmen Marzoni previously had told a psychiatrist at a nearby State institution that the blue-eyed girl was certain the hypnotist was psychotic.
6. The murdered girl and the hypnotist both were orphans.

Though this is all he had to go on, Fordney quickly identified the slain girl. Can you?

Who is the murdered girl? Turn page for solution.

• • •   NO BEER FOR THE CORPSE   • • •

Clifford McHugh savagely tore the note into bits. There was but one way to handle a blackmailer. Trouble with most people when they get into a jam and have to kill, was their timidity. Their hestitant, faltering strokes betrayed them as they did the unsuccessful forger. He would act with audacity. That saw a man through. No one knew that he knew Dorrance, and, when it was learned that Dorrance was a recently released convict, investigation would be merely routine. It was a cinch.

* * *

Fordney glanced curiously at the interior of the sedan with its blood-soaked rear seat and followed the stretcher into the morgue of the small northern town.

As the corpse, blasted by a shotgun charge, was lifted to a table McHugh said, "I found this man on the old logging road about fifteen miles north of Oakdale. I was driving from my cottage on Black Ghost Lake to town

---

Solution — Mystery in the Dell

In (1 & 2) we learn that the girl who leased the farm is neither Myra Bubley nor Carmen Marzoni. Consequently, neither has blue eyes. Also we see that as Sylvia Lane did not lease the farm, she is not the girl with blue eyes.

Hence the girl who leased the farm is Bernice Sloan. But Bernice is not the dead girl, as the murdered girl has brown eyes and the girl who leased the farm is blue-eyed.

In (4) we observe that Sylvia Lane is neither the dead girl nor the hypnotist.

And it is obvious in (5) that neither Carmen Marzoni nor Bernice Sloan (the blue-eyed girl) is the hypnotist. Therefore Myra Bubley is the hypnotist.

As neither Sylvia Lane nor Bernice Sloan is the dead girl and as the murdered girl was the subject of the hypnotist (Myra Bubley) the murdered girl is Carmen Marzoni.

REASON IS OUR INTELLECTUAL EYE — Shakespeare

---

when my headlights picked him out. I examined him, saw he was dead and brought him here."

"Don't you know that you are not supposed to move a dead body?" roared Police Chief Swanson.

"Certainly!" snapped McHugh, "but the nearest phone is twelve miles. Did you expect me to leave him to the animals?"

The only object in the corpse's pockets was a beer check from a tavern twenty miles from Black Ghost Lake.

"Why didn't you take this man to a doctor?" Fordney asked.

"Why? Because he was dead!"

"What is his name?"

"I never saw him before."

The criminologist studied the beer check. "You're lying," he said quietly.

How did Fordney know? Turn page for solution.

• • • • **THE STEWART AFFAIR** • • • •

"What a night," sighed Professor Fordney as he hung up the telephone receiver. Half an hour later, still grumbling, he splashed his way through the mud and rain to the door of 13 Nelson Road. Removing his rubbers in the spotless vestibule, he stepped into a large, well-furnished living room running the entire width of the house. Introducing himself and explaining he would question everyone later, he asked to be alone.

In the far corner of the room he found a man lying on the floor, his throat cut. As he bent over his attention was attracted to a dime about five feet from the head of the dead man. He picked it up, regarded it curiously and with a thoughtful look put it in his pocket.

The Professor began his questioning with the butler.

"You found the dead man?" he asked.

"Yes, sir. I was returning from posting a letter about twenty minutes ago and just as I was coming up the path to the front door I heard a scream, dashed in, and found Mr. Green gasping his last breath."

"Lose a dime?" inquired Fordney mildly.

"Why, I don't think so, sir," replied the servant nervously feeling his pockets.

"I also heard the scream," volunteered Stewart, owner of the house, "and ran in here from the library, right behind Moxom."

"Did either of you leave this room before I arrived?"

"No," replied Stewart, "we remained here until you came."

"Did you, Mr. Stewart, lose a dime? No? Well," remarked the Professor, "it looks like collusion to me and I can tell you Inspector Kelley won't swallow this story."

What was wrong with it? Turn page for solution.

Solution — No Beer for the Corpse

Had the man been dead when he picked him up, as McHugh alleged, the back seat of his car would not have been blood-soaked. McHugh shot the blackmailer with a shotgun (which he threw in the lake) on the logging road (according to his plan) but instead of waiting for him to die he panicked, put him in the car before he died and while still bleeding profusely, and drove to the morgue.

BOLDNESS IS EVER BLIND — Bacon

The petals of a four leaf clover, which the body of Charles DeLong had pressed against a spot of green in the Oriental rug, did not escape the trained eye of Professor Fordney, and the great criminologist placed it between the pages of a personal letter. He looked down at the knife wound over DeLong's heart.

* * *

"I wish you could remember the exact time you left Adolph Lyon," patiently insisted Fordney. He was questioning Irene Adler in her apartment. "Lyon said you found that four leaf clover and stuck it in his buttonhole for luck. He can't place the time of your walk together in the country, but if you could, it might help his rather weak alibi."

"Adolph found DeLong dead?" exclaimed Irene in a faltering voice.

"That's correct. He says he stepped into DeLong's apartment after leaving you. Upon entering the room, and seeing in a horrified glance that DeLong was obviously dead, he ran immediately to the library, phoned the doctor and police, and there awaited our arrival.

"What are your relations with Lyon?" The Professor's smile relieved the abruptness of the personal question.

"We're engaged. Surely you don't believe him guilty?"

"Well, I wouldn't exactly say that. I had hoped to learn something from you that would clear Lyon of all suspicion. Did you also pick these this afternoon?" Fordney asked, lightly touching the flowers in a vase and removing a dead leaf.

"Yes . . . yes . . . we did. You're not holding Adolph . . . ?"

"For the present—yes."

Why? Turn page for solution.

Why? Turn page for solution.

• • • • • **THE MORRISEY CASE** • • • • •

"I don't know nothin' about his murder," nervously retorted Nell Gillson in reply to Professor Fordney's remark: "You're the first arrest in the Morrisey case." He stepped up and drew her back from the train gate. Just then a passer-by brushed against Nell, knocking her purse to the ground. Fordney, hastily retrieving it, felt a gun in it. No question now about Nell being involved!

* * *

"You've befriended me more 'an once, Professor," old Annie had hiccoughed as she admitted Fordney to her room in the tenement house. "And that's why I sent for you. I just came from Tony's," she whispered with an air of secrecy, "and I heard Nell Gillson havin' an argument with that bum Richards she's been hangin' around with.

Solution — The Stewart Affair

Had the butler dashed in the front door as he said he did there would have been foot tracks in the vestibule as the path leading to the door was muddy. The Professor found the vestibule spotless. Therefore, Moxom, the butler, was lying, and as Mr. Stewart corroborated his story he was also necessarily involved.

NAY, HER FOOT SPEAKS — Shakespeare

He told her to beat it out of town on the 5:20 from Central Station—that he'd meet her there . . ."

"Get to the point, Annie," interrupted Fordney. "You didn't call me . . ."

"The point! They'd just murdered Pat Morrisey in his room!"

"Why in thunder didn't you say so before!" exclaimed the Professor. He hurried to Morrisey's hideout and found the man's bullet-riddled body! Glancing at his watch he discovered he could just make the station in time. And if Annie was right . . .

* * *

"So you don't know anything about the murder, eh?" said the Professor, pocketing Nell Gillson's purse. "Then why signal a tipoff to your pal Richards, who just came out of the waiting room? A confession, Nell, might save you from the chair!"

How did Fordney know Nell was involved in the murder? Turn page for solution.

• • INCIDENT OF THE THREE TROUPERS • •

"You mustn't pay any attention to the weeps of our starry-eyed little chum," one of the trio who followed the Toledo boarding house proprietor, Mrs. Kinsella, up the stairs to the room they had just rented had said. "You see," continued the speaker, "she's a hypnotist's assistant so she's always out of her mind, and when you add love to that, well . . ."

"You don't know which of the other two women said that?" Professor Fordney asked the landlady.

"No, I don't," said Mrs. Kinsella. "The three women, who said they were in show business, gave their names as Daisy Hunt, Clara Walsh, and Wanda Reynor when they

167

asked for a room last night, and I didn't pay any attention to who was who. One of them—kiddingly it seemed to me—made that remark, but I didn't look back so I don't know which one. And I don't know which one of the three it is I found dead in bed this morning. The other two had vanished."

On a crumpled program in the dead woman's suitcase, Fordney found scrawled two pieces of information which, together with the above remark, enabled him to identify the girl who had died from an overdose of Veronal. The scrawled items were to the effect that:

1. Clara Walsh and the hypnotist's assistant had organized an act of their own for which they hoped to get vaudeville booking which would take them to South America.
2. Daisy Hunt and the dead girl broke into vaudeville as dancers ten years ago, while the frequently hypnotized girl had been in show business only two years.

Who is the dead girl? Turn page for solution.

Solution — A Weak Alibi

Fordney wanted a satisfactory explanation of why the four leaf clover was under DeLong's body. Lyon definitely implied he had not touched the body. If he had not, how did the clover get there? The young man was later found guilty of the murder.

Solution — The Morrisey Case

When Fordney said, "You're the first arrest in the Morrisey case," Nell replied, "I don't know nothin' about his murder!" Had she not possessed at least guilty knowledge of the affair she could not have known that Morrisey had been murdered.

THE GHOSTLY CONSCIOUSNESS OF WRONG — Carlyle

Professor Fordney walked into the cottage and found Inspector Kelley reclining in a deck chair. "I'm all in, Joe," Kelley sighed. "Not a sign of a breeze all day and this humidity is terrible! Where have you been?"

"You missed the excitement. Murder's been done!" Fordney rejoined.

"Where? When?" without enthusiasm.

"Couple of hours ago. Peters's body was discovered down near Britton's landing by a fellow named Hart. The river's about half a mile wide for quite a stretch along there, and rather desolate. Hart said he was moving slowly upstream watching the shore through binoculars when he saw Peters. Anchoring his sailboat in midstream he came ashore in a dinghy. I was with Sheriff Cass when he reported it.

"Cass was quite excited . . . his first murder case. Peters had been shot in the forehead, but from my examination I'd venture a guess he was drowned first." There was no response from the deck chair. The Professor continued:

"Hart was eager to assist. He pointed out the peculiar position of the body, footprints along the bank, and marks showing signs of a struggle. He made no comment about the absence of blood, however.

"When I asked to see his binoculars he nervously replied he had dropped them overboard in his haste. Cass didn't realize the preposterousness of Hart's story at first but when he did . . . Say, Kelley! Are you listenin'?"

A refined snore broke the silence and with a sigh Fordney stretched, yawned luxuriously and joined his friend.

Why did Cass arrest Hart? Turn page for solution.

"There," Ed Burke patted the sand with a spade, "is the finish of a perfect job. Neat, too, wasn't it, honey? That rat Dyer had it coming."

"Yeah, a nice clean job, Ed," Clara Miller agreed. "But don't ever forget that I saw you drop him."

* * *

Sergeant Reynolds carefully lifted the gun from the hole, shook the sand from it, hurried to headquarters, and placed it on Captain Wiley's desk.

Wiley swung round; the Professor lit a cigar.

Solution — Incident of the Three Troupers

Let's first discover who the hypnotist's assistant is. 1. She is not Clara Walsh. 2. She is not Daisy Hunt; therefore she is Wanda Reynor. Daisy Hunt (2) and the dead girl had been in vaudeville for ten years, while Wanda had been in only two years; as neither of them is the dead girl, she must, perforce, be Clara Walsh.

READ TO WEIGH AND CONSIDER — Bacon

Solution — Are You Listenin'?

A boat cannot sail upstream without "a sign of a breeze." This was what Hart said he did.

THE WIND BREATHES NOT, AND THE WAVE WALKS SOFTLY AS ABOVE A GRAVE — Bailey

"It's the chair for Burke if this gun checks with the bullets from Dyer's body," said the captain.

"It will," Clara assured him.

"For you too, Clara, if you were with him."

"I wasn't! He told me he did the job and where he buried the rod on Braxler's Beach."

"But why are you turning in Burke now—four months after the killing?"

"Because," blazed the girl, "the louse has been two-timing me for months! I just found it out. That's why I told you where the gun was. Nobody's double-timin' Clara!"

Fordney reached over, shook a few grains of sand from the glistening barrel of the wicked-looking .38 caliber revolver and broke it. There were four cartridges in the chamber. Dyer was shot but once.

"Have you an alibi for Dyer's murder?" inquired the Professor.

"Sure. I was with Jimmy O'Leary."

"Did Burke give you a map, or merely tell you where he buried the gun?"

"He just told."

"Quite. Better lock her up, Captain," Fordney suggested. "Don't know her game yet, but obviously she is lying."

How did the Professor know Clara was lying? Turn page for solution.

"What a fog!" muttered Hale Spence as Dodge, his manservant, took his damp wraps. "Had to walk from the club . . . couldn't get a cab at any price. Got lost twice . . . you couldn't see your hand in front of your face! Get Billings on the phone. Bradwell's . . ."

"Pardon me, sir, you have a visitor . . . A Professor Fordney . . . ."

"Hello, Spence," greeted the criminologist. "I overheard your conversation. As a native Londoner you shouldn't mind this weather!"

Spence's face clearly indicated he was not pleased at having a caller, but his: "Won't you join me in a drink?" was cordial.

Fifteen minutes later he was aware of the purpose of Fordney's visit. Scotland Yard, suspicious of Spence's connection with a counterfeiting ring, had asked Professor

---

Solution — Murder in Two-Two Time

Had the gun been buried in sand for four months, its barrel would not have been glistening. As a hold on Burke, Clara dug up the gun the day after he buried it. Later becoming tired of him and afraid he would kill her if she left him, she reburied the revolver in the same spot and immediately notified the police where it could be found. Clara is serving a long sentence; Burke is doing life.

A CLEVER WOMAN OFTEN COMPROMISES HER HUSBAND; A STUPID WOMAN ONLY COMPROMISES HERSELF — Talleyrand

Fordney to interview him. Through subtle inquiries he learned far more than his host was aware of.

"The Yard was about to arrest Bradwell as head of the ring, but he was murdered this afternoon," casually remarked Fordney.

Spence stared through half-open lids. "Yes. So I learned on my way home from the club. Saw the headlines of an evening paper as I passed a newsboy about a block from the flat. But let me tell you, Professor, the Yard's mistaken! Bradwell conducted a perfectly legitimate business in Tottenham Court Road. I've bought several antiques from him."

"Is this one of them?" inquired Fordney, indicating a chair.

"Yes, it is. Why?"

"If you are not involved in Bradwell's murder you will have no objections to telling me, honestly, how you knew he was dead!" sternly stated Fordney.

Why was the criminologist suspicious of Spence? Turn page for solution.

* * * * * * * **CLASS DAY** * * * * * * *

"Morning, lads," beamed the Professor as he entered the classroom accompanied by a slight, dark, distinguished-looking man of fifty. "I've brought quite a celebrity with me. Boys, meet Inspector Marcel Guidont of the famed French Sûreté. Inspector, my young hopefuls."

Introductions acknowledged, the Professor continued. "M. Guidont is properly known as the greatest homicide detective on the Continent, and is head of the Sûreté's renowned school of criminology. I've told him what bright lads you are, but he is an extremely skeptical gentleman so I brought him along to prove it to him. M. Guidont has come over to assist me in the investigation of the murder of that beautiful young Parisian. You remember—the girl who won the international beauty contest recently at Coney Island.

"Perhaps," continued Fordney, "I should apologize to the Inspector for the simplicity of the little problem I am going to ask you to solve for him, but . . ."

"Do not disturb yourself," smiled the Frenchman. "And I have an idea, mon ami! Suppose we invite the young gentleman who solves your problem first to work with us on the LaLonde case!" A shout of approval went up from the class.

"It's a deal!" agreed the Professor. "Ready? Here's the problem: A friend of mine in the country recently received a generous offer for the property on which he had built a modest bungalow. As he liked the house and owned another piece of property not too far distant, he decided to move it. After some difficulty the movers got the bungalow on a large log three feet in circumference—on a gentle down-grade. The question is, had my friend pushed the log himself, how far would the house have traveled while the log made one revolution? Quickly now!"

What is your answer? Turn page for solution.

Solution — The Professor Wonders

Spence could not have seen the headlines in the fog. He was later convicted as one of the counterfeit ring.

INCONSISTENCY WITH OURSELVES IS THE GREAT WEAKNESS OF HUMAN NATURE — Addison

---

Three men were picked up recently in a floating sea-plane by the Coast Guard boat RELIANCE. They had radioed shore two days previously, stating they had been forced down but apparently did not know their position, so attempts at rescue had been unsuccessful until Captain Cowan, commander of the RELIANCE, had spotted the plane off the Virginia Coast.

He found two of the men unconscious and the third in a delirium. Although brought to shore as quickly as possible, the two unconscious men died. The third was still unable to talk coherently when Professor Fordney was asked to help in their identification. He learned the three were Charles Diamond, Harold Sellstrom and Christian Volimer. But who was who?

Among their papers was an unsigned agreement of sale of the plane from the owner to Harold Sellstrom.

The Professor's investigations of the mystery led to the discovery that the three were soldiers of fortune attempting a secret flight from America to Dakar. He also learned the following:

Diamond was recently divorced.

Before taking off the owner of the plane expressed his jealousy of the living man over his attentions to his (the owner's) sweetheart.

The surviving member thereon threatened to quit the trip, but as he was the only experienced pilot, Diamond prevailed upon him to come along.

Diamond also said that if the owner continued his tirade the pilot was likely to throw him out of the plane when they got over the ocean.

With only the above information, Fordney quickly identified the living man.

Who was he? Turn page for solution.

"I got back to our lodge not more than ten minutes after Alice did," lamented Harold Sherrod, "but I was too late—too late! She was already dead!"

"Take it easy, young man—I realize how difficult it is, but you must pull yourself together," said Fordney. "There—that's better."

"We'd been hunting together east of the lake," Sherrod went on. "Suddenly my wife seemed to tire and said she thought she'd go back. Knowing she would find her way all right I had no hesitancy in having her go alone. I told her I'd be back in a couple of hours, but shortly after she left me thoughts of her suicide threats entered my mind. I tried to dispel them as she had been so cheerful the past month. They persisted, however, and I began to worry

---

Solution — Class Day

The house would not have moved at all!

Solution — An Easy Identification

The Professor learned, as you probably did, that Sellstrom was not the owner of the plane; that Diamond was neither owner nor pilot, therefore Volimer was the owner. He also ascertained that Volimer and Diamond were the dead men; Sellstrom the survivor.

IF I GO TO HEAVEN I WANT TO TAKE MY REASON WITH ME — Ingersoll

and become uneasy. Call it premonition if you like, but there it was—a feeling that something definitely was wrong!

"My appetite for hunting gone, I set out for the lodge and there I found her dead—a bullet through the temple— my revolver beside her. She had done it after all!" sobbed the man.

"See anyone from the time you started back to the lodge until you called the police?"

"Not a soul. It's lonely country."

"How far away were you?"

"Roughly, between two and three miles."

"Surprising you didn't overtake your wife. Would you object to a test on the polygraph—the lie-detector, Sherrod?"

"No—why should I?"

"Why? Because while I know you are lying, I warn you the polygraph will confirm it!"

Why did Fordney believe Sherrod to be implicated in his wife's death? Turn page for solution.

Turn page for solution.

• • • THE STORY OF PETE MONAHAN • • •

"Pete Monahan," said Professor Fordney, "had been tipped off that his brother was being brought back from the south under guard on a charge of embezzlement in Philadelphia. He even knew the car number, and that his brother and the guards would be riding in the drawing room.

"He hastened down to Wilmington, the last stop before Philadelphia, and after buying a ticket to Philadelphia, paced impatiently up and down the platform in the cold, driving November rain.

"As the train approached the station the torrent was intensified, but that meant little to Pete—he was out to save his brother. Having previously learned where car 62-B would probably stop, he drew back into the station doorway as the train came to a halt.

"Beside a drawing room window of 62-B he saw the heavy, stern countenance of his brother's guard. Next to the law slouched his brother, dark circles under his eyes, and a hopeless, strained expression on his face. Confident he had not been observed by either, Pete dashed through the rain to the Pullman car behind, pushed aside a startled porter and mounted the steps. He had about forty minutes before the train reached Philadelphia. He must think fast and act fast. He did both! Once they were well under way he . . ."

"We asked for one of your own crime cases, Joe," interrupted a fellow club member, "and you're up to your old tricks—even an old codger like myself can spot the fallacy in that one!"

What was it? Turn page for solution.

Solution — The Premonition

Had Sherrod been entirely innocent there would have been no reason for him to have made the statement that he arrived at the lodge ten minutes after his wife, when he could not possibly have known at what time she did arrive! This one little slip started him on his way to the gallows.

IN GENERAL, TREACHERY, THO' AT FIRST SUFFICIENTLY CAUTIOUS, YET IN THE END BETRAYS ITSELF — Livy

The underworld was not surprised. They had been expecting it. Foxy Louis Chapin had lost his cunning. And when he went out of his way to taunt the Feds, underworld wise money was giving odds on his sudden demise. The wise money won. Foxy Chapin's butchered body was found on the city dump.

Chapin headed a state-wide black market mob which was mulcting millions from thousands whose appetite was stronger than patriotism. The others of this unsavory mixture of brains and brawn, terror and tact were: Abe Wolstein; Andy Ritter; Hap Traynor; Moose Maloney; Tom Drake; Gyp Bangor; Sig Donaper and Viv Salvari.

Asked by his old friend, Inspector Kelley, to assist in the homicide hunt, Professor Fordney painstakingly assembled the following facts:

1. Wolstein, Traynor and Chapin's murderer controlled the poultry end of the ring's operations.
2. One of the eight was an army deserter. This was known only to himself, Drake and Donaper.
3. A week before the murder Salvari, Bangor, Wolstein and the deserter met with black market operators from Chicago. Maloney was incensed when told of the outcome.
4. Two days before the killing Ritter, Drake and the killer demanded that Chapin pull in his lines, stop extending the ring's scope and desist from all further cop-baiting. When Chapin sneeringly refused, Ritter, the killer and the deserter beat him up.
5. The day of the murder Bangor, Salvari and the killer talked over murder plans with Maloney. Maloney agreed to spot Chapin for the kill.

Nine days later the entire gang was rounded up.

Who was the killer? Who the deserter? Turn page for solution.

Solution — The Story of Pete Monahan

It would have been impossible for Pete, in a driving rain, to have observed through the car window from his position at the station, the dark circles under his brother's eyes; not to mention the expression on his countenance!

Solution — Death in the Black Market

Wolstein was not the killer (1) or the deserter (3).

Ritter was neither killer nor deserter (4).

Traynor is eliminated as the murderer (1).

Maloney was not the deserter (3) or the killer (5).

Drake was neither deserter (2) nor killer (4).

Bangor was not the deserter (3) or the murderer (5).

Donaper was not the deserter (2).

Salvari was not the deserter (3) or the murderer (5).

Consequently Traynor, eliminated only as the killer (1), was the deserter and Donaper, eliminated only as the deserter (2), was the killer.

WHAT'S IN A NAME? — Shakespeare